NED BUSTARD
Squalls Before War:
HIS MAJESTY'S SCHOONER
SULTANA

NED BUSTARD
Squalls Before War:
HIS MAJESTY'S SCHOONER
SULTANA

Veritas Press, Lancaster, Pennsylvania
©2006 by Veritas Press
800-922-5082
www.VeritasPress.com
ISBN-10: 1-932168-27-3
ISBN-13: 978-1-932168-27-3

Watercolor paintings, pen and ink illustrations
by Marc Castelli [www.marc-castelli.com]

Photographs by Lucian Niemeyer

All rights reserved. No part of this book may be reproduced without permission from Veritas Press, except by a reviewer who may quote brief passages in a review; nor may any part of this book be reproduced, stored in a retrieval system or transmitted in any form by any means, electronic, mechanical, photocopying, recording or otherwise, without prior permission from Veritas Press.

Printed in the United States of America.

*This book is dedicated to
the crew of the schooner* Sultana
—both past and present.

Contents

	NOTE	ix
I.	OVERBOARD	1
II.	LIBERTY	13
III.	MERMAID	23
IV.	DEFIANCE	37
V.	CHESAPEAKE	51
VI.	MADNESS	63
VII.	WASHINGTON	77
VIII.	PEACE	87
IX.	POLLY	101
X.	KING GEORGE	115
XI.	CAROLINA	131
XII.	GASPEE	143
	EPILOGUE	159
	ACKNOWLEDGMENTS	161
	GLOSSARY	163

A Note Before Reading

Some readers have asked if this book is fiction or history. It is both—it's fictionalized history. The plot of this book does not tell of a great romance, mighty war or treacherous quest. It merely follows the work of a boat enforcing the laws of the Crown in the middle of the eighteenth century. The sailors aboard the *Sultana* did not know that they were sailing in the headwaters of war or that they were playing a part in the formation of a new nation. They were just doing their job. *Squalls Before War* is a slice of history—showing the excitement and tedium of life on a schooner between 1768 and 1772.

One of the appealing aspects of writing a fictional account about the tour of His Majesty's Schooner *Sultana* is the fact that the entire logs of both Lieutenant Inglis and Master Bruce have been preserved. We know exactly where the schooner was and what it was doing as it patrolled the colonies' waterways. These logs have at the very top of the page the month and year, with each entry listing the day of the week and the date, along with boxes for wind directions, courses, distance in miles, latitude, longitude, bearing and distance at noon and, finally, comments. Since there is a great amount of repetition in these entries—and most modern readers will find them cryptic—the full date and comments are usually all that will be found in this book. And for readability, some spelling irregularities have been corrected.

Overboard

A STORM WAS BREWING, AND MASTER DAVID Bruce was none too happy about it. It had already been a rough crossing, and it looked as if circumstances were not going to improve in the immediate future. He scanned the horizon, his green eyes set in a weather-beaten face topped with unruly chestnut hair that seemed perpetually windblown. The schooner's master wore a long overcoat against the foul weather. Beneath it he wore a once-white vest and his blue officer's coat—for warmth rather than duty. Topping things off, he wore a crumpled, wide-brimmed canvas hat covered with tar for weather-proofing.

"Mr. Huxley, I suggest going below," Bruce absentmindedly encouraged the surgeon's mate. The poor fellow was looking ill and was sure to be a hindrance as the weather worsened. What on earth possessed him to follow a life at sea since he was so clearly unsuited? He seemed to fall ill more than his patients, and a less cheery fellow would be hard to find. "Bo'sun, please have the foretop sail dropped," Bruce ordered. "I am going below to speak with the Lieutenant."

"Drop the foretop," acknowledged Joshua Lowe, the boatswain's mate on duty that watch. Then he called forward, "Drop the foretop, ya Corkers!" Two young Irishmen responded by jumping to the rat lines, climbing up the fore shrouds. "Drop the foretop," they parroted.

David Bruce stepped off the poop deck to slide the aft grated hatch off and turned to descend the steep ladder into the lower level of the schooner. An experienced sailor, Bruce had served as boatswain on the *Lynx* in '61, and then also later on the *Lively,* before joining the crew of His Majesty's Armed Schooner *Sultana* at Deptford Dock on the eighteenth of July. As the master of the *Sultana,* Bruce was primarily in charge of navigation and served as second-in-command, directly below the captain of the ship—Lieutenant John Inglis—on whose door he knocked.

"Come," a voice barked from within the Lieutenant's cabin in response. "Ah, David, it's you. I was going over the charts, and you've made some miscalculations. It seems we are somewhere between the Alleghenies and the Mississippi River," John Inglis grinned.

"Well, then it is a good thing the late war with the French is over and that region belongs to England and not France," David replied. David was a much better navigator than the lieutenant due to a quicker mind mathematically—yielding a recurring joke about miscalculation. "I wish your readings were truer than mine, as I would certainly desire to find ourselves closer to land. We are about to encounter a bit of a blow."

"Ah, now I wish you *were* joking with me. But after that hard squall last Thursday, such a jest would be in bad taste. Well, lead on my friend, and we'll see what the heavens wish to bestow."

Inglis slipped into his dark blue navy lieutenant's coat with nine gold buttons running along each wide, white lapel and placed his fore-and-aft bicorn hat on his head before following Bruce back up to the helm. The wind was blustering, and the sky had changed quickly from a rumpled, gray blanket to a boiling menace of dark clouds.

All the humor drained from the Lieutenant's face. Inglis was an austere-looking man at most times, with dark hair combed to the side and charcoal eyes set beneath imposing eyebrows. He had a long, aristocratic nose with a small mouth set above a slightly cleft chin. "Reef the main," the lieutenant commanded.

"Aye aye, Lieutenant," replied the boatswain, and he relayed the order, "Reef the main!"

The schooner became a fury of activity as the Lieutenant's orders were carried out. Looking forward from where Bruce and Inglis stood, the deck was mired down with rigging, the gig and twelve half-hogsheads of beer lashed to the rails. The schooner sailed on, the rain parting like a curtain as they entered the storm. The rain intensified as if offended by the sailors' impudence in attempting to climb into the rigging. Draped over the yards, the men began tying up the sail using bits of rope that had been sown into the sail for this purpose. Once they were done, the sails' overall area was reduced, causing the schooner to heel less.

"Keep us sailing close to the wind," Bruce urged the man at the helm as the schooner continued to be blown about.

"Man the bilges," Inglis ordered.

Bruce automatically passed the order along. "Deal and Clark—man the bilges." Able-bodied seamen James Clark and John Deal acknowledged their orders and climbed back over the half-hogsheads to reach the bilge pump. Lightning broke the sky as James and John began pumping on either side of the main mast. Foul water spewed out of the ship's hold, joining the torrents from the sky which were flowing over the side of the schooner.

Bruce called down through the grating in the aft hatch to the ship's clerk. "Mr. Dearl, how are we doing down there?"

A wiry man peered up from the gloom and replied, "Half the Atlantic is down here, but we're holding our own."

And the *Sultana* continued to persevere as they sailed into the night—there was no sunset, just gloom begetting blackness. The hull continued to creak and groan as the waves buffeted her and seamen shouted and struggled to reset slipping lines. Time seemed to stop as they crashed on and on through the dark storm.

After what seemed like days of relentless rain, Bruce muttered, "I believe the wind has changed."

"I suppose we should have expected as much," Inglis replied. "The sea's been quite the cheeky mistress tonight—constancy from the wind would certainly be too much to expect." Then to the two seamen struggling to hold the tiller, he ordered, "Take us a few points off to the south." The *Sultana* altered course so that the wind wasn't blowing into her bow.

Now either the men at the helm overcompensated or the sea pushed harder against the schooner. Regardless, she was off course, with the result that the small ship was at the wrong place at the wrong time and a giant wave rose over the *Sultana*. Instead of the schooner cutting through it, a huge wave came crashing down on her midship. Both Inglis and Bruce were thrown against the rails, and the *Sultana* seemed to disappear under the sea. When the water had run off, Deal and Clark who had been manning the pump were crumpled farther down against the same railing. Bruce leaped to their aid.

"Are you two alright?" he yelled. At that moment lightning exploded across the sky. David saw the blood on Deal just before darkness fell again on him. The storm had been having a temporary blinding effect like that on them all throughout the night. "Clark, get Deal below—see if Mr. Huxley can help him."

"Moffet—Ritchie," bellowed Inglis. "Roundly now, to the bilges!"

Coughing and spluttering from the sea's recent assault, the two seamen climbed aft to pump.

"I'm surprised we're still afloat after that," said Bruce.

"If you can call this still afloat," retorted Inglis. "I feel like now we are sitting at water level."

Clark climbed back up on deck and confirmed the Lieutenant's hunch by interjecting, "Sir, our supplies in the hold are *floating*."

"Thank you, Mr. Clark."

"What about Deal?" queried Bruce.

"He smashed his ear, Master Bruce—it appears that there is more blood than damage."

"Faster on those bilges," Inglis exclaimed. But the bilges could not empty the hold faster than the water was pouring in. The water inside the vessel was forcing the *Sultana's* bow down, thereby throwing the ship's center of gravity too far forward. The result was that the tiny vessel was alternating between having her rudder pulled out of the water and having her bow dip so low that each wave she encountered was crashing over into the boat and filling the hold more.

"Drop the top sails," Inglis ordered. The acknowledgement of the orders was just heard over the din of the storm, and several sailors went aloft.

"Stay sharp up there," Inglis yelled to the seamen aloft, "I have no wish to lose our topsail yards again like we did in that storm last week!" It seemed a small eternity before the sails were finally brought down. No noticeable change occurred, so Inglis ordered a second reef on mizzen and called for the jib to be reefed.

Bruce was helping to stow the sails with the help of a sullen sixteen-year-old able-bodied seaman Edward Cunningham and the Lieutenant's servant, eight-year-old Christopher Curtis.

"Master Bruce, why don't the Lieutenant bring all the sails down instead of tying 'em up like that?" asked the freckled boy. "Don't the sails just make the wind push us over more?"

"It's not 'tying up,' Chris—it is called 'reefing,'" David Bruce distractedly explained. "And we need the sails up to continue to make way—if not we will find ourselves at the mercy of the sea."

"Drop rear sail—triple reef the mizzen!" Bruce heard Inglis cry out as he climbed out of the hatch onto the wildly pitching deck. He could picture in his mind's eye the soaked forms above him in the darkness, swinging in the rigging, fulfilling the lieutenant's instructions.

"Lieutenant, Clark wasn't stretching the truth much about the hold—it is as wet down there as it is up here!"

"I'm not surprised," Inglis answered. The ship lurched and the bow sank beneath another hill of water.

"I think we need to set the storm jib," Bruce suggested as the deck once again fell away from them, the *Sultana* heeling suddenly to port.

"My thoughts as well," Inglis said, standing on the poop deck with legs bent to accommodate the pitch, as one would do on an inclined roof. "Drop the jib—set the storm jib!"

Bruce amplified the orders, "Nichollson—give Jurd a hand up there!"

John Jurd, a handsome young sailor from London who was surprisingly at home at sea, straddled the bowsprit, inching out towards the blocks ten feet forward of the bow. When he was halfway out, a hole opened in the sea and the *Sultana* fell into it.

"Hold on," yelled the Norwegian Nichollson as a wave swept across the bow, pummeling all within its path. When the schooner broke free of the deluge, the norseman called again, "John, are you still there?"

Lightning charged across the sky, illuminating the miserable lump that was able-bodied seaman Jurd. He was clinging for dear life to the slender shaft of wood and was only able to moan in response. But quickly he resumed his journey to the schooner's farthest outpost.

"Ready," croaked Jurd as another wave threatened to remove him from his roost. With Jurd in place, the order was given to proceed with dropping the jib. Jurd's job was to "hank on"— unhook the metal loops from the forestay and pass the canvas back. As soon as the large mass of canvas was removed, Nichollson began feeding a smaller triangle of canvas up to Jurd, who then proceeded to hank on the storm jib.

"That should keep us making way," Inglis said hopefully to no one in particular. Jurd was able to get back on board with slightly less trouble than when he set out, and the storm seemed to begin to cooperate.

"Let's get some of you tars in the hold with buckets," ordered Bruce. "We need to help Moffet and Ritchie empty us out!" The two Scotsmen had continued to labor at the bilges—a task that was almost comical in its futility—for nearly an hour. Several sailors struggled below as the *Sultana* continued to heave and pitch.

Farther and farther over the schooner rolled. With each swell the water inside the schooner rushed up the sides, knocking her on her beam. And with each roll she also stayed heeled over longer and longer.

"Much more of this and we won't be able to right her," Inglis grimly said, stating the obvious as he hung on to the binnacle to keep standing. Just before Bruce was able to reply, unnatural daylight cracked off the stern, making the shadows of the lieutenant and the master leap across the midship stores that were lashed to the deck.

"The beer," they said to each other simultaneously.

"All hands on deck!" And as if realizing that Inglis and Bruce had thought of a way out of its trap, the storm rallied and began blowing the rain across the ship, rather than just drenching them from above.

"Untie the half-hogsheads of beer midship and roll them overboard," bawled Inglis. There seemed to be a slight pause as the concept sunk into their collective minds, then they tore into the task with a vengeance.

"Master Bruce, why are we throwing away all those supplies?" asked young Curtis. He had come up on deck with the others and was huddled near Bruce, by the *Sultana's* main mast.

"The schooner is top heavy, Chris, and each time wind or wave pushes her over, the water that has been rising steadily in the hold aggravates that. Those twelve half-hogsheads of beer weigh well over two tons—when we are free of them, the schooner will drain more quickly and not take on water so fast because she will ride higher in the water. Now get on down below—this is going to be hard work."

It sounds like a simple task to set barrels on their sides and roll them into the sea. Yet with the deck heaving up and down like a crazed colt intent on bucking a rider, and the sheer weight of the cargo swishing around inside, it took six men to move each barrel. Two stood in front of it with staves to keep it from rolling too fast in one direction, and the others put all their strength into shoving the barrel in the right direction. There were passing complaints about throwing away good alcohol, and others expressing deep concern about dying of thirst if the rest of the trip took longer than expected, but all of these were lost beneath the howling of the wind and the groans of the men as they labored. It was two hours before all the barrels were overboard and nearly another before Inglis and Bruce felt they could leave the deck in the hands of the bo'sun. By then the storm was only miserable instead of completely terrifying.

John Inglis and David Bruce entered the aft cabin and stripped off their outer coats in a vain attempt to dry off. Inglis sat down at his desk and pulled out his log, commenting, "I'm very grateful for the way the men carried out their orders during this storm—such loyalty is a treasure in the Service."

"Loyalty?" Bruce said in surprise as he collapsed on the settee. "I suppose you could call it that . . . the desire to live can certainly serve as a motivating factor in birthing 'loyalty' and 'devotion.'"

Later that evening, Lieutenant Inglis got out his quill and daily log to record that day's events: "Strong gales and squally with rain . . ."

Inglis Logbook:

September 13, 1768. Strong gales and squally with rain brought too under the foresail. Shipped great deal of sea. Obliged to heave overboard into the sea 12 half-hogsheads of beer to save the schooner from foundering.

Liberty

On Monday, the twenty-fourth of October, 1768, the sky was a flawless blue and Halifax Harbor was crisp and clear as it cut into the shoreline of Nova Scotia. In stark contrast to the beauty of that fall day, the *Sultana* shuffled into port, tired and haggard from her hazardous crossing of the Atlantic.

The weary crew guided the *Sultana* past the *Martin*, the *Zephyr* and the *Viper* to find a spot to drop anchor off St. George's Island. She looked very tired and small beside the ten-gun, 100-man *Viper*.

Originally, the *Sultana* had been a schooner rig ship with only five sails, but when she was purchased and refitted for service in the Royal Navy to enforce the Townshend Acts in the colonies, two top masts were added so she could carry more sail for speed and maneuverability. "Mr. Dearl!" the Lieutenant shouted above the din of the crew stowing loose lines and tidying the ship for its time in port.

"Yes, Lieutenant?" The *Sultana's* clerk poked his head out from the forward hatch. William Dearl, a transfer from the *HMS Achilles,* was the ship's clerk, the man responsible for all the provisions to be found on board the schooner.

"Mr. Dearl, please take the launch into Halifax and begin to replenish our supplies at the Victualling Office." The Royal Navy had a Victualling Board that purchased the food and issued it to the various ships in the fleet at victualling offices in various ports, including Halifax. "Take Ritchie, Jurd and Grant with you, along with our good surgeon, Mr. Huxley," Inglis continued. Then as an afterthought Inglis smiled and said, "And have young master Curtis join you." The Lieutenant's servant was an energetic boy and the youngest son of friends of the Inglis's family in England. The crossing had sobered him a great deal, but he still had the enthusiasm of an army, and visiting the port would be a good channel for it.

The clerk set out and the crew continued its laborious resuscitation of the schooner until mid-morning when the boatswain called out, "Ship off the port stern."

Lieutenant John Inglis stared through his scope then snapped, "That is Commodore Samuel Hood's *Launceston*. Mr. Smith, prepare the guns for a thirteen-gun salute on my command." The gunner's mate leaped into the nether regions of the ship to fulfill his orders.

The *Sultana* had been fitted with eight half-pound swivel guns when the Navy had overhauled her for her new service. The gunner and several ship mates placed the small-bore cannons into the gun stanchions. As the *Launceston* glided by the *Sultana,* Inglis yelled, "Fire!" and, with precision gained from practice at sea on the trip from England, the cannons went off, one after the other in succession, with five being reloaded and fired again. The *Launceston* returned the salute before anchoring nearby.

"Ah, that's showing the colonials the *proper* way to respect one of His Majesty's vessels," Bruce said softly as the two senior officers of the *Sultana* witnessed the exchange. After their gruelling crossing, all seemed right again with the world. He understood his duty in the Service and his obligation to the Crown. The Navy was anchored right there before his eyes as a glittering testimony to his allegiance.

"I suspect that half of our mission over here will be to teach the locals what fidelity and respect look like," Inglis agreed. The Lieutenant went below to retrieve dispatches from England in his cabin and then was rowed over to the *Launceston.* By midday four and a half tons of water had been brought on board, and the Lieutenant had returned from the *Launceston.*

Once he was settled, Inglis called Bruce out of his cabin and into his own. At the foot of the aft ladder was the

surgeon's mates' cabin opposite Bruce's, with the Lieutenant's beside it, farthest aft. There was an unusual layout of men's cabins extending forward with four on either side. More than just hammocks yet not nearly as comfortable as the officer's cabins, they were small beds like large cabinets with sliding wooden doors. Each of the eight cubicles was an average of six feet long and three wide with just over two feet of head room. The hold was filled with a mass of sails and barrels and crates, leaving only enough space between the fore and aft hatches for the crew to crawl. Inglis was sitting on the settee built in along the back of the cabin, filling his pipe with tobacco, as Bruce entered.

"How did your meeting go with Commodore Hood?" Bruce queried. Seeing the posture of the Lieutenant, David settled into the chair by the desk that they used for keeping their logs, as it appeared they would be having a long talk. The cabin was roomy in comparison to the rest of the boat, with just over five feet of head room. A bunk was built into the port hull, and the whole space was lit from two windows on either side of the boat and three across the stern above the settee.

"Very well, thank you. Hood inquired into our passage then launched into a lengthy update on the state of affairs in the colonies," Inglis said before lighting his pipe. "Tell me David, what had you heard about Boston before we left Deptford?"

"I understood that this past spring the tensions between radicals and officials of the Crown were heating up, due in large part to the Townshend Acts," Bruce replied.

"Yes, that had been my understanding as well. Yet it turns out that over the summer Boston has been beset with virtual mob rule. The Crown officers all reported that 'a general spirit of insurrection was prevailing throughout the province.'"

"Just because of the Townshend Acts? That seems a bit of an overreaction to a small duty placed on tea, glass and such," said Bruce.

"It appears that the fuse was lit by an incident that began this past April. One of New England's wealthiest citizens—and a leading critic of the Crown's policies—Mr. John Hancock, had his ship the *Lydia* boarded by two customs officials. Would you believe that the firebrand forcibly removed the servants of the King and had them taken to shore!"

"How did he think he could get away with that?"

"Oh, Hancock claimed that they had 'a lack of proper authorization,'" Inglis said mockingly. "Criminal charges were quickly filed of course, but they were later dropped when it was determined that the officials had not secured writs of assistance to allow the search."

"Well, then it was resolved according to the law. I can't see why that would stir things up in Boston to the degree you've implied," Bruce said while beginning to sharpen a quill.

"That incident alone would have been fine, I'm sure, but on the tenth of June, customs seized his sloop, the *Liberty,* because its cargo of Madeira wine had been unloaded without going through customs. And the warship *Romney* was ordered to tow the *Liberty* away from Hancock's dock to the harbor to prevent a rescue attempt. Then the Sons of Liberty—"

"Sons of what?" interrupted Bruce.

"'Sons of Liberty'—that's the name the local malcontents are taking. These groups are popping up all over. Back in '65 Isaac Barré referred to the opponents of the Stamp Act as the 'Sons of Liberty,' and now these secret groups have adopted the name. It's been used before, by a variety of local rabble-rousers, but these new incarnations consist largely of well-to-do and respectable artisans, merchants and gentlemen. These groups actually *organize* uprisings, and they will not hesitate to use violence to advance their agenda," Inglis explained between puffs on his pipe. "Anyway, the Sons of Liberty stirred up a mob gathered on the wharf, and they pelted the custom house officers with stones and other missiles and attacked the customs house. The mob broke windows and dragged a small boat belonging to one of the collectors through the city and made it the central element in a huge bonfire on the Common!"

"Were any of the customs officials injured during the event?" Bruce inquired.

"No, they wisely fled to Castle William—the island fortress in Boston Harbor. But it wasn't over. Three days later the Sons of Liberty held a meeting at Faneuil Hall and appointed a committee to petition Governor Francis Bernard for the removal of the *Romney*. The next day the Governor promised to do all within his power to fix the situation. I understand he said, 'I shall think myself most highly honored if I can be, in the lowest degree, an instrument in preserving a perfect conciliation between you and the parent state."'

"An overly courteous response to the ruffians, I'd say."

"Quite so. And then he even promised to end impressment."

"End press gangs?" Bruce burst out incredulously. "And I suppose he can put an end to hiccups as well? How does he think the navy will stay manned? Able-bodied seamen don't just spring full-grown from the ocean. No one likes the press, but until recruitment includes a chest of gold for each man, it's a fact of life."

"Certainly, Bernard couldn't make good on his promises," Inglis replied. He took a long draw on his pipe, blew out the smoke, and continued. "Now all the while this was going on, he was also secretly trying to get troops into Boston, either from New York or England. Then later, London ordered the governor to appear before the Massachusetts assembly and call for the revocation of a letter that had been sent last winter to the other colonies calling for united resistance to the Townshend Acts. Ninety-two members voted against the governor and only seventeen voted for."

"So then we shouldn't expect to be invited to dinner by any of the Massachusetts assembly?" Bruce asked with a smirk.

"I'd say not!" Inglis laughed. "But the assembly doesn't exist anymore. The Governor dissolved the assembly in July, and it has been chaos there since. Personally, I don't think the Commodore likes the customs commissioners down there, but he is officially giving them his full support. Therefore, we are going to help in the deployment of troops as soon as we can make ready."

"After spending the last month battling wind and wave a mere one hundred leagues from shore, we are going to set sail again? The crew will be overjoyed," Bruce said facetiously.

"I am sure. Which makes this a perfect time to read the Articles of War again." The Articles of War were originally established over a century earlier and served as the "holy writ" for naval life. They were read at least once a month on a Sunday after the church services. They were also read when punishment was executed. "We need to remind everyone of their duties to the Crown—and of the consequences for disobedience," Inglis grimly muttered.

INGLIS LOGBOOK:

October 24, 1768 Moor'd in Halifax Harbour. Light breezes with calms, hoisted out our boat, emp'd rowing the schooner into Halifax Harbour. Came too in 10 fathoms water, found riding here His Majesty's Sloop Viper, arrived here His Majesty's Ship Lancestance. Read the Articles of War to the Schooner Company. Fired to salute Commodore Hood 13 guns

Mermaid

BOSTON BOILED WITH UNEQUIVOCAL FURY. His Majesty's armed schooners *St. Lawrence* and *Sultana* quietly joined His Majesty's warships *Beaver, Bonatta, Glasgow, Romney, Senegal,* and *Mermaid*. Within a few days the crew of the *Sultana* was aiding in the transport of the Sixty-fourth and Sixty-fifth Regiments of British soldiers from the navy vessels into the city. It was Commodore Samuel Hood's intent that the Townshend Acts be enforced and malcontents put in their place by the Crown's sheer display of force.

"Mr. Lowe, please have the ship's boat pulled around," David Bruce ordered the boatswain. The rain was falling, and the dreary weather foretold of a long mundane day of work ahead of them. Lowe repeated the Master's orders to a pair of seamen. The ship's boat, a cutter, trailed the *Sultana* off her stern—she was eighteen feet long, about six feet wide, fore-and-aft-rigged for rowing or sailing and was used for carrying heavy weights of men or stores.

"Cunningham, Lowe, Ritchie and Caton—you will be joining me on the first transports today," Bruce informed them. Then turning to the Lieutenant's servant said, "Curtis, please drop below and inform the Reefer that we are prepared to begin. He is to relieve me on this watch."

The young boy scurried down the ladder to fetch the 'Reefer,' that is, the midshipman. James Sutherland, a nineteen year-old Scotsman, quickly attired himself in his stiff-collared, blue midshipman's coat for work topside, and in a few moments the cutter was being manned.

"So, Joshua, you're having a bit of a homecoming today, eh?" Bruce asked the boatswain as the men settled into their places at the oars that were staggered throughout the cutter.

"Aye, sir, that I am," replied Lowe as he grabbed onto the *Sultana's* main shrouds to ease himself down into the cutter. "But I hardly recognize the place, to be honest. I was born here around thirty years ago, but besides changes in the number of buildings . . . well, when I was a child here we were a bit—shall we say—more *hospitable* to visitors."

"Yes, I see that the crowd on the docks don't remember those friendly times. I imagine they don't care for England sending shiploads of soldiers to them to house and feed," Bruce rejoined. "Cunningham, you'll have to keep a lookout to see if you see any friends of yours among the soldiers—I understand the regiments consist almost entirely of your Irish brothers."

"That would be grand, Mr. Bruce," Edward Cunningham replied, "but I'd be more eager to set foot on solid ground."

"Ah, if we were to set foot in Boston, I could take you tars to a grand spot called the Midwood Tavern," Lowe added wistfully, "And a lovely lass named Lydia used to serve there."

"I can't imagine that tavern is worth a court martial for desertion, though. Cast off, Mr. Cunningham," ordered David Bruce as the rain began to fall heavily.

The wind blew out of the northwest, adding miserably to the rain. The *Sultana's* cutter joined the small transports in creaking and crashing against the sides of the large ships bearing the soldiers. One by one the soggy soldiers climbed down into the cutter, and *Sultana's* men rowed them to the wharf. It had been since the fourteenth of June that the customs commissioners in Boston had been waiting for these troops. They had fled to the Castle William for asylum when faced with rioting mobs of colonists. They insisted that it would be impossible for them to step foot in the city without two or three regiments occupying the city. They also would maintain their self-imposed exile until they had the assurance from the civil authorities they would call for troops whenever the customs officers felt the need for extra protection.

On their third ferry of the *Sultana's* cutter across the harbor, one of the soldiers found the weather did not impede his tongue and chatted merrily with the seamen.

"Cor! I am glad to be off that floating prison," the infantryman prattled on. "Two blessed months in that ship—and the weather did not once give up. I declare I now know what it feels like to *really* be pickled. Why back in Blarney—"

"Blarney? Why, I grew up in county Cork," Cunningham chimed in. "But I must say you have no idea what cooped up is like until you have spent four months—and a day!—on a wee boat as I have been serving on. It's the smallest schooner in the fleet, and when it is filled with supplies there is precious little more room in it's hellish hold than to crawl." The two then compared memories of old haunts, both roomy and snug.

Soon they reached the wharf, and Cunningham jumped onto the wharf to tie off the lines for the cutter. To empty the boat was a tedious process, as each red-clad soldier attempted to get onto the wharf in one piece with all the equipment he carried with him—musket, musket balls, bayonet and a knapsack with blankets and camping gear.

"We don't want you lobsterbacks here!" shouted a young boy from the dock. "Go home, bloodybacks!" added a woman further back in the crowd. As had been occurring all day, townsfolk crowded around offering impolite and often rude remarks, getting in the way to make the process of unloading the soldiers as difficult as possible, without outright defiance. Eventually the soldiers were off and the men from the *Sultana* had returned to their oars.

"Cast off," Bruce said while gazing through the rain at the ships in the harbor. "Ed, did you hear—?" Turning, he saw the boat was missing one sailor. Roused out of their drudgery-inspired malaise, the others then noticed his absence as well.

"Where did Cunningham go?" "He was just here a moment ago, I'd swear." "Is that him over there?" Each man was up and looking about, nearly capsizing the cutter. Master Bruce then walked up and down the wharf twice before returning in defeat.

"Cast off, Joshua," Bruce sighed. "Cunningham seems to have gotten his wish to set his foot on solid ground. I wonder how lucky the Irish really are? For his sake, he better make his next wish that I never find him." Bruce stared back at the wharf for a while, before picking up again on his diatribe as if he had only paused for a breath. "It is the audacious self-centeredness of it all. As if his individual desires trumped his duties and obligations. I must say that it pushes me beyond the scope of my imagination how someone could be so cavalier about their responsibilities. And after all we went through together on the crossing ... oh, the Lieutenant will be livid, that's for certain."

INGLIS LOGBOOK:

November 16, 1768. Moored in Boston harbor, the Long Wharf WSW one Cable's length. First part Moderate & Cloudy with Rain. Middle & Later parts Strong Gales & Cloudy. At 7 am Manned Ship for General Gage Going on board of the Romney as did all the Ships of the Fleet. The Boats employed in Landing the Troops out of the transports

"Article fifteen of the Articles of War clearly states that: 'Every person in or belonging to the fleet, who shall desert to the enemy, pirate, or rebel, or run away with any of His Majesty's ships or vessels of war, or any ordnance, ammunition, stores, or provision belonging thereto, to the weakening of the service, or yield up the same cowardly or treacherously to the enemy, pirate, or rebel, being convicted of any such offense by the sentence of the court martial, shall suffer death.'" The voice of the captain of the HMS *Mermaid*—a 28-gun, 200-man frigate—rang out across the harbor. All hands of the *Sultana*, along with those on the other ships in the harbor were on deck to witness the execution of the punishment that had been handed down.

"Able-Bodied Seamen Robert Bignall and Thomas Dean have been convicted of attempting to desert from this, His Majesty's Ship the *Mermaid*, and so will be whipped 'round the fleet,'" the captain continued.

Slowly the two men were placed into separate launches and their wrists were tied to capstan bars above their heads so their bare backs were clearly exposed. The two boats bearing the guilty men were rowed beside each of the ships in the harbor. Drums beat out as the cat-o'-nine-tails ripped into the backs of Bignall and Dean ten times alongside each ship.

The launch bearing Bignall was first to bump against the starboard side of the *Sultana*. Bruce obediently stared down to watch the punishment resume. The sailor's back was already a mass of slices and bruises. Toward the center of his back the skin had been ripped away and steam rose in the cold November air as the blood flowed down, soaking the waist of his trousers.

One, two, three, four lashes were issued. The sailor meting out the punishment rested his arm for a moment and resumed. Five, six, seven, eight, nine, ten—the cat-o'-nine-tails was nothing now but a crimson confusion. The launch moved on to the next ship and was replaced alongside the *Sultana* by the boat bearing Dean. After the launches were rowed past several other ships, the men of the *Sultana* were dismissed to resume their normal duties. Inglis invited Bruce into his cabin, and the two shared some brandy.

"Well, I can't imagine those two seamen will be called 'able-bodied' any longer," the Lieutenant said grimly, breaking the silence between them.

"Maimed for life, I'd say," agreed David. "But I suppose they didn't fare as badly as the *Mermaid's* quartermaster, Odnall. He is going to hang a few days from today, correct?"

"That was what was *said* at the court martial, but between you, me and the deep blue sea—I expect to see Mr. Tom Odnall given a reprieve."

"Aw, that's bilge water!" Bruce protested.

"I wouldn't put money on it, but that was my reading of things. It really is too bad that things should get to this and that all three of them couldn't just have been given two dozen of the best and been done with it. But trying to run in such a conspicuous spot as Boston—"

"And with the political scene as tense as it is right now," Bruce interrupted.

"Yes, of course under these circumstances the full force of the law had to be displayed." Inglis finished his brandy and looked out the windows in the stern of his cabin. "Yes, it is too bad ... especially since I dare say that we've all wanted to 'swallow the anchor' over the years. Did I ever tell you about when I deserted?"

"No! I would not have fancied you'd be the sort to run," David exclaimed.

"I was fourteen when I joined the Navy. I was serving on the

HMS *Garland*—a fine 20-gun ship with a crew of about one hundred and sixty men. But Arbuthnot—the captain—was a coarse, blustering, foul-mouthed bully. I eventually came to the point when I could not tolerate his temper any longer. So while we were moored off the coast of Virginia, I relieved Captain Marriott Arbuthnot of one more whipping boy."

"So how did you get back into our 'fashionable' society?"

"My family had some connections, and I was able to serve under Captain John Elliot on the *Aeolus*. Then at eighteen I was rated a midshipman and things took off during the late war."

"Speaking of the French conflict, did I ever tell you about my tour on the *Lively* when we took the *Valeur*?"

"I'd say if I had a sixpence for every time you've told me about it, I'd own my own fleet of *Sultana's*!" Inglis laughed.

On the sixth of December the *Sultana* was ordered to sail south with His Majesty's Sloop *Senegal* to continue enforcing the Townshend Acts in the waters around Rhode Island. They arrived several days later in Newport's harbor under a veil of snow.

A week passed, and then on a bright and clear Christmas Day the *Sultana* was patrolling the inlets along the coast of

Newport. As the *Sultana* rounded Castle Hill Point about mid-afternoon, southwest of Newport harbor, the wind shifted to a heading from west to northwest and the hand aloft spotted a square-rigged, two-masted ship to the lee of Goat Island.

"Mr. Bruce, does that strike you an odd lay for a winter berthing?" Inglis asked Bruce rhetorically.

"Quite curious. Are we going to acquaint ourselves with them?" Bruce replied in equal jest, his hand at the tiller. Then he added, "With the sun behind us, we may be invisible to them as we beat up toward the ship."

"My thoughts exactly," Inglis answered. Raising his spyglass, the Lieutenant was able to read the insignia, *Royal Charlotte*, in sea-stained letters, gold gilt and slightly peeling. "We have them 'cabined, cribbed, confined'—to quote *Macbeth*. Our approach cuts off the harbor as an exit for them, leaving their only hope of flight into the wind to the north."

"Of course, this assumes a near perfect setting of the anchor in concert with the backing of the mizzen and top sails," Bruce reminded Inglis.

"I have every confidence in you, Master Bruce," Inglis grinned before bellowing, "Ship's company, prepare to board!"

The *Sultana* passed the *Royal Charlotte* by almost a ship's length before the Lieutenant cried, "Let go the anchor!" followed by "Douse all sails!" The sails spilled their wind, and the schooner drifted alongside of the *Royal Charlotte*.

Several boarding lines were cast over, and Sutherland, ever the overachiever, abruptly jumped over the side and onto the *Royal Charlotte's* deck. This was unfortunate, as he toppled onto one of the *Royal Charlotte's* deck hands and a small brawl ensued. Inglis stepped over in the wake of several of his crew and said quietly, "Mr. Sutherland, that is quite enough—consider your flimsy," referring to the certificate of good character and leadership a midshipman needed for promotion. Then loudly he addressed the captain of the brig: "Sir, you appear to be unloading cargo here. May I see your papers?"

"The officer from the custom house has . . . already been on board—yesterday," the shifty man answered.

"Then may I see the documents you showed to him?" Inglis pressed.

"I didn't—that is—he was persuaded that—rather, he was compensated to such a level that he asked to be put ashore."

"I see. Sadly for you, captain, the servants of the Crown aboard the *Sultana* are not able to be bribed. Mr. Sutherland, stay aboard the *Royal Charlotte*—and Ritchie, Clark and Grant as well. Nail all of the hatches closed. We are seizing this ship according to the rules of maritime law," ordered Inglis.

MERMAID

INGLIS LOGBOOK:

December 25, 1768. Newport Harbor. Moderate & Clear. Seized the Royal Charlotte Brig with 6 Cases of Gin. At 2 past went on board the Brig & Found the Customhouse officer on Shore. Seized the Brig with all her tackling & Left an officer on board with 3 men & nailed up her hatches for Benefit of his Majesty & heirs.

The *Royal Charlotte* was the source of a great deal of conflict over the next two months. The custom house and the schooner had overlapping spheres of jurisdiction, so there were bound to be conflicts of interest. Despite the deplorable actions of the custom house officer, the Newport Custom House and the *Sultana* both filed claims against the *Royal Charlotte*. In the end, the legal costs rose so high that neither party profited, with only the gin being condemned.

Defiance

*J*OHN HUXLEY WAS DEAD.

In one way, the loss of Mr. Huxley was not so terribly great, as he was a rotten sailor and never did seem to get his sea legs. No, the dilemma was that Huxley was the only surgeon's mate the *Sultana* had, and every ship needed a good surgeon—regardless of his nautical aptitudes.

The *Sultana* had been sailing in the waters around Newport on the twenty-fourth of February, 1769, when the surgeon's mate gave up the ghost. The freezing, wet weather they were experiencing greatly heightened the impact the illness would have had in more hospitable climes. On the following day Huxley was laid to rest in Newport's common burial ground, burials at sea being avoided when possible.

Following worship services on Sunday, the twenty-sixth, the crew had lingered around the mast as the last of the surgeon's mate's clothes were auctioned off to cover the cost of his burial.

"Thank you, Mr. Dearl," Inglis said at the end of the auctioning. Then turning to the boatswain on duty ordered, "Mr. Lowe, please see to the ice that has collected on the rigging overnight."

"Aye, sir," replied Joshua Lowe before conveying the orders to two of the seamen on deck.

It was a clear morning, and the wind was picking up as the *Sultana* began to work her way up to Providence. David Bruce appeared from below and offered Inglis one of the pair of steaming mugs that he carried with him to the poop deck.

"Thank you very much, David. Just the thing for a morning like this," the Lieutenant said as he received the beverage gratefully. "It doesn't look like there will be many boardings today."

"No, I imagine breaking their boats free from the ice is a bit of a deterrent," Bruce answered.

"Rhode Island certainly has earned its reputation as a hotbed for smugglers, but perhaps not as warm as the smuggler's own beds," Inglis smiled. "You have to wonder if our former chancellor of the exchequer 'Champagne Charlie' Townshend had any clue that his Townshend Acts

SULTANA

to solve the problems of imperial finances would meet with such heated defiance by the colonists."

"Oh, I am sure he didn't. The riots at the time in England impressed upon him the need of tax relief. All his thoughts were focussed on reducing the national debt by taxing the colonies," said David Bruce.

"Which makes sense, since England invested so much money in the war with the French on their behalf," said Inglis as he stopped to enjoy the descent of a few hot sips to his belly. "He had wagered that the colonists wouldn't bristle at an external tax since their previous objection to the Stamp Act was attributed to the fact that it was an internal tax."

"I can at least sympathize with those in New York who would find the Restraining Act unpalatable, since it suspended permission for their assembly to meet due to their position on the Quartering Act of '65," Bruce said and then conceded, "And perhaps they were asked to shoulder the lion's share of providing basic necessities for British troops stationed within their borders."

"Well, I don't know about that, but the reorganization of the customs service shouldn't have been difficult to swallow. And creating and headquartering the new Board of Customs Commissioners in Boston just makes sense, due to the intense resistance there to the Acts of Trade. Also, I agree that new admiralty courts were necessary to have in Boston, Philadelphia and Charleston—Halifax is really too far away to be truly effective."

"I imagine that taxing imported paint, paper, glass, lead and tea is probably not the problem with the colonists, but rather the clear intent of the Townshend Duty Act to bypass the traditional role of the assemblies to pay the salaries of royal officials in the colonies. It's a power struggle."

"Sadly, it seems that the fact that this is all for the good of our country appears to have gone unnoticed," Inglis growled as he emptied his cup.

"So now the colonists are echoing Saint Paul: '. . . the commandment, which was ordained to life, I found to be unto death,'" mused Bruce. "And now we are Townshend's hand of justice, carrying out his will—even as he lies in the grave."

Inglis laughed and said, "I wonder if where he is, he is dealing with worse hotbeds and ice than we are!"

INGLIS LOGBOOK:

February 26, 1769. First parts moderate and clear latter fresh breezes. Emp'd working up to Providence. At 1/2 past 3 pm struck on a bank Providence Island SbW 2 miles Squash Point SSE 3 miles. Came to anchor in three fathoms water

The sun was high on the first of April, and a crisp wind toyed with the rigging as the *Sultana* sat merrily at anchor in Rhode Island Harbor. Bruce looked over larboard, saw their ship's boat approaching with one more man on board than when they had left. David called, "Mr. Dearl, you appear to have come home with your hands full!"

"I was concerned with the escape of so many crew members recently, that there would be no one to eat this bread I was going ashore to purchase," Dearl replied with a grin.

"I'm David Bruce, the *Sultana's* Master," Bruce offered as he reached a hand down to help a graying negro to get on board.

"My name is Prince Gould," the man replied as he took Bruce's hand. The ship's clerk came up next, and James Clark began to hand up the bread and other supplies.

"How old are you, Gould?" Bruce continued.

"Two score and five, and an able-bodied seaman since I was a boy," Gould said with pride.

"Well, that will make you the senior of our crew," said Bruce. Then his attention was caught by a splintered oar in the boat below. "What happened to that?" he demanded of William.

Instead Clark confessed, "That would be my fault, sir. I

was using the oar to help us shove off back on shore and seemed to have gotten it caught under a rock, and it snapped."

"By the look of it, the oar had already had a fracture of some kind to make it break like that," Bruce suggested. "I'll report it to the Lieutenant later." David Bruce's head snapped back to what was happening on board as Prince Gould cried out and bent double on the deck under the load he had been lifting out of the cutter. "What is it, Gould?" he asked the black man.

"I have a right sharp pain in my side, sir. I won't lie; it has been troublin' me some time now. Mostly it is manageable, but then other times..."

"Have you ever had any experience cooking, Prince?" Bruce began to lead the man forward as Gould replied, "Oh yes, I was the ship's cook for my whole duty on the ship I served on before last."

"Good—we lost our last cook just recently. And I am sure you will do much better than he did in the post. You have no idea how poorly a bloke can cook when he wants to leave. Our last *real* cook was from Bermuda—John Mudge was his name. We've had others fill in since then, but few have shown much skill." Bruce stopped talking to push away the forward hatch, and the two men descended to find themselves right before the stove. The stove looked like a small fireplace with an iron cap that had a stovepipe sticking out of it. The raised brick hearth was big enough to accommodate one large pot. "Now the bread brought along with you today used to get stored up here, but the bread room was knocked down and rebuilt in the stern by our carpenter's mate just a few months ago. Rats had been getting to it, and Lieutenant Inglis thought moving it aft would help solve that problem." Bruce continued to show him around the mess, giving him his bearings. Then Gould was signed into the muster and given new slops by Dearl.

INGLIS LOGBOOK:

April 1, 1769. Moored in Rhode Island Harbor. Fresh breezes. Received from the Senegal half a Cord of Wood. Broke one of the boat oars by Accident. Prince Gould, a black man entered on board.

The *Sultana* resumed its regular rounds in the Newport area, searching ships with a vigilant eye for signs of smuggling. On the first of March, in the midst of gales with hail, a twenty-seven-year-old Scotch carpenter by the name of John Phillips was added to the logs. Two days later John

Haliburton enlisted. Also hailing from Scotland, the thirty-year-old, quick-witted Presbyterian filled the cabin opposite David Bruce's but most importantly filled the vacant post of surgeon's mate. Unlike the departed Mr. Huxley, Haliburton enjoyed life on board ship and healed with laughter as much as with medicines. March and April was spent about the bay, with periodic returns to Newport.

That spring several young men were pressed into service aboard the *Sultana,* but in spite of fine sailing weather, their stay was short and they ran as soon as the opportunity arose.

Not all who joined the *Sultana* needed to be coerced. Seamen had an incentive to volunteer rather than be pressed. Volunteers could choose the ship they wanted to serve on, and at the very least, signing into the Royal Navy was a way to escape poverty, boredom or a bad marriage. On the first of June, just before Lieutenant Inglis received new orders to sail south, another Scot volunteered—Thomas Nichollson, a twenty-eight-year-old gunner whose experience quickly saw him taking over the responsibilities from the seaman who had been struggling to fill the post since Deptford. Nichollson tended to have a shorter fuse than most, but he was nigh-maniacally focused on details and soon had the shot locker and all things explosive orderly and well in hand.

On a Friday afternoon in the beginning of July, Thomas Nichollson had his first opportunity to exercise his pyrotechnic gifts. The cannons had been fired before, whenever the crew of the *Sultana* needed to stop a ship to board it and search for contraband. They had been doing this since they first arrived in Halifax in 1768. But this time it was a matter of honor.

"Mr. Nichollson, bring your wares to the fore deck," a testy Lieutenant bellowed through the grating in the quarter deck hatch into the hold below. "Grant! Please give Nichollson the assistance he requires. You may begin by moving this cannon by me to a post in the bow." Inglis's command was not impossible for a lone sailor to accomplish—due to the small size of the *Sultana,* she carried only small swivel cannons.

Charles Grant hopped to attention and proceeded to lift the cannon out of the post that held it and cradled it like a baby as he navigated the ropes, gig and other clutter on the deck. The *Sultana* had six posts on the fore deck extending above the railing, and into the center of one of these Grant slid home the metal shaft of the cannon. Then he gave the cannon a half turn back and forth using the long cord-wrapped handle that trailed off the cannon like an inverted handle to a frying pan.

The gunner's mate was soon there and saw what had raised the ire of the Lieutenant. A merchant's brig was sailing up past the *Sultana* with a pendant flying, thereby showing a great deal of cheek. Proper naval etiquette dictated that Navy vessels ran a pendant at the mast head to identify it, and for this ship to do the same could only cause confusion at best. In this situation, it was a base act of condescending disrespect.

"Mr. Nichollson, fire a shot off that brig's bow to teach it some manners," Inglis barked. "No matter what our size, we are one of His Majesty's ships and will not be insulted in this fashion." The rhythmic noises of the *Sultana* on the river were broken by a sharp punch of sound and the whistle of lead flying through the air and splashing well in front of the offending brig. When the merchant continued on unruffled,

Inglis muttered, "Colonial maggot." Then he called to the gunner's mate, "Fire again, Tom, and this time aim for the pendant!"

The gunner's mate acknowledged the order and quickly shot another piece of hot lead screaming through the July sky. A cheer and laughter erupted from the crew of the small schooner as some of the merchant brig's rigging shattered and half the pendant was torn away, quickly inspiring the offending craft to strike the remaining shreds.

"Lieutenant," the surgeon's mate said, "it looks like the falling rigging may have injured one of the sailors on that brig. Do you want to send me over in the gig to see if we can help?"

"I should think not," Inglis replied instantly. "We'd be round the bend to aid such a perfidious lot as that."

"Pardon me sir, but they are fellow servants of the Crown and—"

"No, they are impudent old tars that need to be taught what their duties are to His Majesty's schooners," Inglis retorted.

John Haliburton's usually sunny face clouded over. "Lieutenant Inglis, those men are created in the image of God just as we ourselves are, and furthermore, His Word commands us to love our neighbor—"

"If we are going to make an appeal to Holy Writ, Mr. Haliburton, the Scriptures are clear—*'Let every soul be subject unto the higher powers. For there is no power but of*

God: the powers that be are ordained of God. Whosoever therefore resisteth the power, resisteth the ordinance of God: and they that resist shall receive to themselves damnation.' Really, I thought you were the ship's surgeon, not its vicar." Inglis stormed down to his cabin. The surgeon's mate was left fuming, and the *Sultana's* Master was left shocked—both that such a light-hearted man as Haliburton would speak so strongly to a commanding officer, and that Inglis would seem so heartless.

INGLIS LOGBOOK:

July 6, 1769 Anchored in Hampton Road. Light breezes and cloudy weather, at 2 pm fired 2 half pounders both shott to make her strike a pendant she had hoisted, at 6 pm weighed and came to sail, at 7 came to anchor in 4 fathoms water, Jewel's Point NbE 2 miles, boarded the Henceford sloop bound to Antigua.

The remainder of July melted away without incident, though they searched many ships, and in August the ship and her crew spent seventeen days in Halifax getting refitted and well-stocked with new supplies. The *Sultana* was back in New York by September, with the only excitement being the unintentional loss of her cutter for a day.

On the twelfth of September they anchored by the HMS *Hussar* at Sandy Hook, New Jersey, under the gaze of a nine-story octagonal lighthouse that was built of rubble and crowned in copper. Inglis and Bruce stood by the binnacle and watched as the sun sparkled off the water and the many buttons of the young man who was rowed over from the *Hussar* that afternoon. Twenty-year-old William Piddle climbed on board, saluting John Inglis and immediately presenting his papers.

"Welcome aboard, Midshipman," Inglis said, returning his salute. "We lost our last young midshipman to the *Ramilles* in Halifax last August. I hope you will stay with us for quite some time, benefitting—I am sure—from your service to the Crown, as we seek to keep these ungrateful colonists in line."

Chesapeake

*B*LACKBEARD'S OLD HAUNTS WERE FAST becoming only a faint memory. The *Sultana* had taken a quick trip to the Carolinas and was now wending her way back north to the glistening waters of the Chesapeake Bay. The Lieutenant's servant, young Curtis, was leaning over the rail, watching the foam drift lazily along the sides of the ship. His attention was suddenly drawn to a dark shape below, moving along with them, and he realized it was the shadow of the *Sultana* on the bay's bed. "Master Bruce?" he called.

"Yes, Chris, what is it?" Bruce replied.

"I think I see the bottom—we aren't in danger of running aground, are we?"

"That is definitely a possibility—we need to stay sharp as

the mouth of the Bay is a notoriously tricky entrance. Many ships have run aground here, but I don't think that we'll find ourselves on the putty today. Though it is about time we check again," Bruce said as he looked over the boy's shoulder. Then David turned to Charles Grant, an able-bodied seaman who had come on board two days before the *Royal Charlotte* incident in Rhode Island, and called, "Grant, heave the lead, would you?"

"Aye, heave the lead," the dark-skinned seaman said, acknowledging the order.

Grant proceeded to tie off a line which had on the opposing end a *dipsey*—a long cylinder of lead weighing well over thirty pounds. Gathering up the remaining line, the sailor began to swing the dipsey like a pendulum several times then swung it around his head like David of old and released it out towards the unseen Goliath ahead of the schooner. The line played out, and as they caught up with it, Grant pulled it in. The depth of the water was determined by counting how many strips of faded blue cloth, tied on the line at intervals, had been submerged. The cloth was tied on at two, three, five, seven, ten, thirteen, fifteen, seventeen and twenty fathoms.

"Two and a quarter five," Grant reported.

"My these waters are clear. We will be fine here, Chris," the Master reassured the boy. "The *Sultana* only draws about eight feet, and Grant said we have that, and almost ten more to spare." Curtis was being bred up to the sea life, and this was his first tour in waters so far from home.

"There are other things we need to be on the lookout for besides shoals," Master Bruce said to the boy and pointed towards shore, asking, "What do you make out those white mounds above the water's edge to be?"

"I'd say they were oysters, but that would not make much sense, would it, since they are out of the water?" Curtis offered.

"Actually, you are right on both points. They are oysters, and even though it is low tide, you wouldn't expect to see them, but these waters teem with them to the point that they can be seen above the waterline at this time of day. Some oyster banks are so large that they actually appear on our nautical charts."

"There must be pretty big oysters to make those banks," Curtis observed.

"Oh, yes," agreed Bruce. "They are much larger than those we have in England. In fact, I have seen some thirteen inches long! At ebb tide the locals row to the beds and with iron-tipped wooden tongs pinch them together tightly down near the bottom, and pull or tear up that which has been seized."

"So the colonists just keep picking them, and the oysters keep coming back?"

"They do—they're like the manna of the Bay. I seriously doubt that even many generations of oyster gatherers could choke off this Providential product," Bruce said confidently. He found it a delight to see the world through Curtis's eyes. Bruce looked forward to what other fresh perspectives he would have on this tour of the colonies.

The fall burned out in a radiant display of color along the shores of the Chesapeake as the *Sultana* patrolled the waters in the vicinities of Norfolk, Hampton, Jamestown, Yorktown and Williamsburg.

The *Sultana* was at anchor after a day of intercepting shipping traffic up and down the James River. David Bruce looked up from his work at the binnacle to see the ship's boat returning with supplies.

Bruce called over the side to the ship's clerk, "So what do you have for us, Will?"

"Among other things, we have four quarters of fresh beef. But to be honest, I nearly expected to be quartered *myself* this afternoon when I went to make some purchases at Merriman's General Store. I was making small talk with one of the other customers, and in passing I mentioned the nature of the *Sultana's* duties," said Dearl. Then he continued with uncharacteristic animation, "And without so much as a

warning shot, I was given an ear-full of the gentleman's thoughts on the Townshend Acts, my lineage and the mental faculties of our King! Thankfully the shopkeeper's daughter—Felicity, I believe she said her name was—interrupted that man's tirade to show me pine soap they had for sale there."

"To wash that other bloke's mouth out, I suppose?" Bruce jested. "Well, we've been hostilely received from the moment we arrived in Boston. It shouldn't be much of a surprise for you."

"Certainly, but the stakes are getting raised quite a bit. Now it looks like the law is getting involved," Dearl continued, beginning to act out his news as he shared it with Bruce. "Over a pint at the Raleigh Tavern, I learned that back in May the House of Burgesses decided that the 'sole right of imposing taxes' on the folks of this colony is 'now, and ever has been, legally and constitutionally vested in the House of Burgesses,'" the clerk said in a drawl with his chest puffed out and thumbs notched in the arm holes of an invisible vest.

Bruce laughed, "So then the *Sultana's* labors are disdained, at least."

"Oh, I imagine it wouldn't be so bad if things just ended there," Dearl fell out of character to answer. "But they are also asserting as an 'undoubted privilege' to send circular letters of grievance throughout the colonies and that the possibility of shipping agitators off to England to stand trial is 'highly derogatory of the rights of British subjects.' And when these sentiments were expressed to me, each was punctuated by a fist slamming the table," Dearl reported with a crescendo.

"Funny, I think fellows would have a better trial across the pond than here in some of the travesties that pass for courts," David mused.

"Nothing about politics strike these folks as funny. And nothing seems to stop them on their crusade. When Governor Botetourt dissolved the chamber for its disrespect in protesting the Townshend Acts, its members just met the next day in Raleigh Tavern and agreed to not import British trade goods, luxury items and slaves."

"Ah, if only non-importation meant a lightening of our load—but it is sure to only foretell of more smuggling. Well, the up side is more prizes for us!"

"We can only hope," agreed Dearl. "Oh, something else I learned of interest while I was in Williamsburg was that they have begun to build a new courthouse."

"Really, where?"

"On Duke of Gloucester Street, between the Raleigh Tavern and Bruton Parish Church, opposite the Magazine." The Magazine, a tall, brick, octagonal tower, was built in 1715 to protect the colony's flintlocks, shot, powder, swords and other tools needed to defend against raids, revolts and riots.

"I have to wonder if the residents of Williamsburg are comforted that those hotheads will be in a new courthouse only separated from that gunpowder by the Duke of Gloucester Street."

"Well, that street will at least slow them down... they say that after a good rain, the street is 'ninety-nine feet wide and two feet deep,'" Dearl grinned.

INGLIS LOGBOOK:

December 28, 1769 In James River Fresh breezes and clear weather with strong frost. At 5 am sent the boat to Williamsburg for fresh beef, loos'd sails to dry

December 29, 1769 In James River Fresh breezes & cloudy weather. Rec'd four Quarters fresh beef 383 pounds, weigh'd, and came to sail. At 7 pm came to anchor in five fathoms water, Newport News point ENE 4 Leagues.

It was summer on the Chesapeake, and the *Sultana* was positioned at the mouth of the Potomac River at Smith Point, searching ships as they sailed down the Bay and out into the Atlantic. David Bruce was in one of the *Sultana's* boats with Clark and Ritchie as they rowed out to inspect a weathered brig.

"His Majesty's Schooner *Sultana* requires an inspection of your ship and papers in accord with the Townshend Acts,"

Master Bruce called up as James and Thomas threw up lines to secure their small craft to the brig. Upon boarding, Bruce began his interrogation. "Captain, I am Master David Bruce of His Majesty's Schooner *Sultana* on board your ship by order of the King to enforce 15 Charles II, Chapter 7, An Act for the Encouragement of Trade. Under this Act you are to give notice of your arrival into the colonies within twenty-four hours, identify yourself and your vessel, provide an inventory of your cargo and give proof that the vessel and her crew are British. You must comply with these requirements before unloading your cargo, on pain of losing your vessel, equipment and cargo."

The tall, dark-haired man who was clearly in charge grudgingly replied, "I'm Cerino. This here's the *Sweet Chariot*, with wheat for Philadelphia."

"Ritchie, please go below and investigate to see if what is in the hold matches his cocket," Bruce said as the captain surrendered the *Sweet Chariot's* certified cargo list to the seaman, then asked the captain, "And your port of origin?"

"Chester Town. It's north of St. Michael's—on the Chester River."

"I know of it—on the Eastern Shore. The customs collector there is William Geddes, isn't it?" asked Bruce.

"It is. Both a sea merchant *and* the tax collector—if that isn't the fox guarding the hens . . ." *Sweet Chariot's* captain insinuated. "Not that it matters to *you,* but we have had the wind against us most of our trip—can you speed this up so I can hope to possibly deliver these goods on time?"

"We will get you back on your way as soon as we've done our duty for the King," Bruce sighed. They completed their inspection and instead of rowing back to the *Sultana*, boarded another ship as it was passing between them and the *Sultana*.

"Captain, I am Master David Bruce of His Majesty's Schooner *Sultana* on board your ship by order of the King..." Bruce repeated for what felt like the hundredth time that day—once they had managed to persuade the captain to allow them on board.

"Captain John Swain," a tight-lipped bearded man answered. "The *Missy B* is carrying tobacco from Fairlee Farm, which is on Fairlee Creek, south of Worton Creek and roughly three miles due east of Pooles Island."

"Ah, another from the Eastern Shore—it seems to be my day for that neck of the woods," Bruce offered in a tone encouraging pleasant conversation. Yet there was no tempting the man with civilities. He seemed to have offered all the information he intended to reveal, and the inspection ended as soon as Bruce had completed a follow-up to Ritchie's inspection.

David Bruce and the two able-bodied seamen made their way back to the *Sultana* to be greeted by the smell of fresh-cooked fish. The sailors aboard the schooner had been using a seine net to catch fish while the inspections had been carried out that day.

"The men have had an abundant catch today," Inglis said when Bruce came in to report.

"Yes, the Chesapeake is blessed with abundant riches—but colonists eager to comply with the wishes of the Crown is not one of them!"

INGLIS LOGBOOK:

October 7, 1769. Moored in Hampton Road, Virginia. Strong breezes and Cloudy. Sent the boats to search two Vessels within the Capes. Boarded a brig from Leith with coal bound to Norfolk. Sent the Cutter to Hampton for sweet water & in coming off she was overset & the said water was lost & no part of them could be saved, being some time before the people were Discovered hanging to the boat.

Madness

Freezing rain and snow swept over the *Sultana* and her crew as she bitterly endured the season of Epiphany while moored in the Elizabeth River, near the mouth of the Chesapeake Bay. Not that it had been any more cheery of an Advent either, with able-bodied seaman Daniel Clark drowning in the James River only three days before Christmas. At this time the crew sought any excuse to huddle around the stove, while they spent their times on watch with wood gathering, minor repairs to the ship and even spinning yarn. Indeed, they attempted only five searches the entire month.

Then in February the *Sultana* began to increase the frequency of searches. They were up to a couple searches each day when they switched their moorings to Hungars Harbor on the Eastern Shore. They searched ships there for just over a week and spent the remainder of the month at the entrance to Norfolk Harbor.

On the fifth of March there was a change in the winds.

The *Sultana* left Norfolk to patrol the mouth of the Chesapeake looking for smugglers in the company of the 32-gun Fifth Rate Richmond Class frigate HMS *Boston* and Mermaid Class frigate HMS *Hussar*.

Then on Tuesday, March 20th, 1770, the *Sultana* anchored at Hog Island—across the James River from the creek leading to Williamsburg and slightly downriver from Jamestown. With Grant and Ritchie rowing and Piddle at the tiller, Bruce sat in the bow of the cutter checking his hand gun to insure it was loaded and in working order. He was comfortable with the weapon, but preferred to use it against rogue elements that *attacked* his vessel—rather than having to be concerned that he would need to employ it against people he was bringing *on board*.

"Good afternoon, Master Bruce," called out a robust customs officer, flanked by two red-clad soldiers. Beside them on the dock near the customs house were several dejected looking souls.

"And to you," Bruce answered. "So these are our guests?"

"That they are. This first is John Isleton to be transported by order of the Governor to Philadelphia to stand trial for the

Madness

murder of an Indian along the Pennsylvania frontier. He will be the one to watch—these others are just mad. We have them bound in such a way that they won't be able to hurt themselves or your crew—at least physically. Katherine Morgan, the redhead here, wails like a banshee. Next to her is Margaret Whiting, followed by Matthew Bryan and James Taylor."

"Fine then. Piddle, get Isleton into the boat up by me so I can keep my eye on him," Bruce ordered. "Ritchie, help the midshipman with the rest of these people after you've finished tying up."

"I wouldn't be surprised if you don't find yourselves transporting more northerners to jails and asylums in the coming days. Madness seems to be in the air up there," the court official said to Bruce.

"What do you mean by that, sir," Bruce asked.

"Madness, sir! Haven't you heard about the chaos going on in Boston this month?"

"Boston was an unstable city when we last were in port, but I hadn't learned of anything recently. What have you heard?"

"The papers are full of accounts of a extremely violent action, two weeks from yesterday. Of course, can these colonial papers really be trusted? They seem to only be filled with puffery these days. Anyway, I can only tell you what I read: It is said that just after nine o'clock on the evening of March fifth, a number of unarmed youths were set upon by twelve soldiers of the Crown with drawn cutlasses, clubs and bayonets."

"I find that very hard to believe," interjected Bruce.

"That isn't the worst of it. On hearing the noise, one Samuel Atwood came up to see what was the matter; and entering the alley from dock square, heard the latter part of the combat; and when the boys had dispersed he met the soldiers rushing down the alley towards the square and asked them if they intended to murder people, to which they answered, 'Yes, by God, root and branch!' and then struck Mr. Atwood with a club. Then Captain Thomas Preston and his men came from the main guard to the commissioner's house and took their place by the custom house. Sadly, some from the town then threw snowballs at the soldiers. On this, the Captain commanded them, 'Damn you, fire, be the consequence what it will!' The soldiers fired successively till eleven guns were discharged. In the end three men were laid dead on the spot and two more struggling for life. And it is said that our troops tried to fire upon or push with their bayonets the persons who undertook to remove the slain and wounded!"

"This is madness," Bruce said vehemently. "Surely, this can not be true." The *Sultana's* master was scrutinizing the customs officer to decide if he could trust the word of this man.

"As I said, I only can speak of what I have read in the *Gazette*. Though I am worried that some will want to take out their anger at the events on *this* custom house," the custom

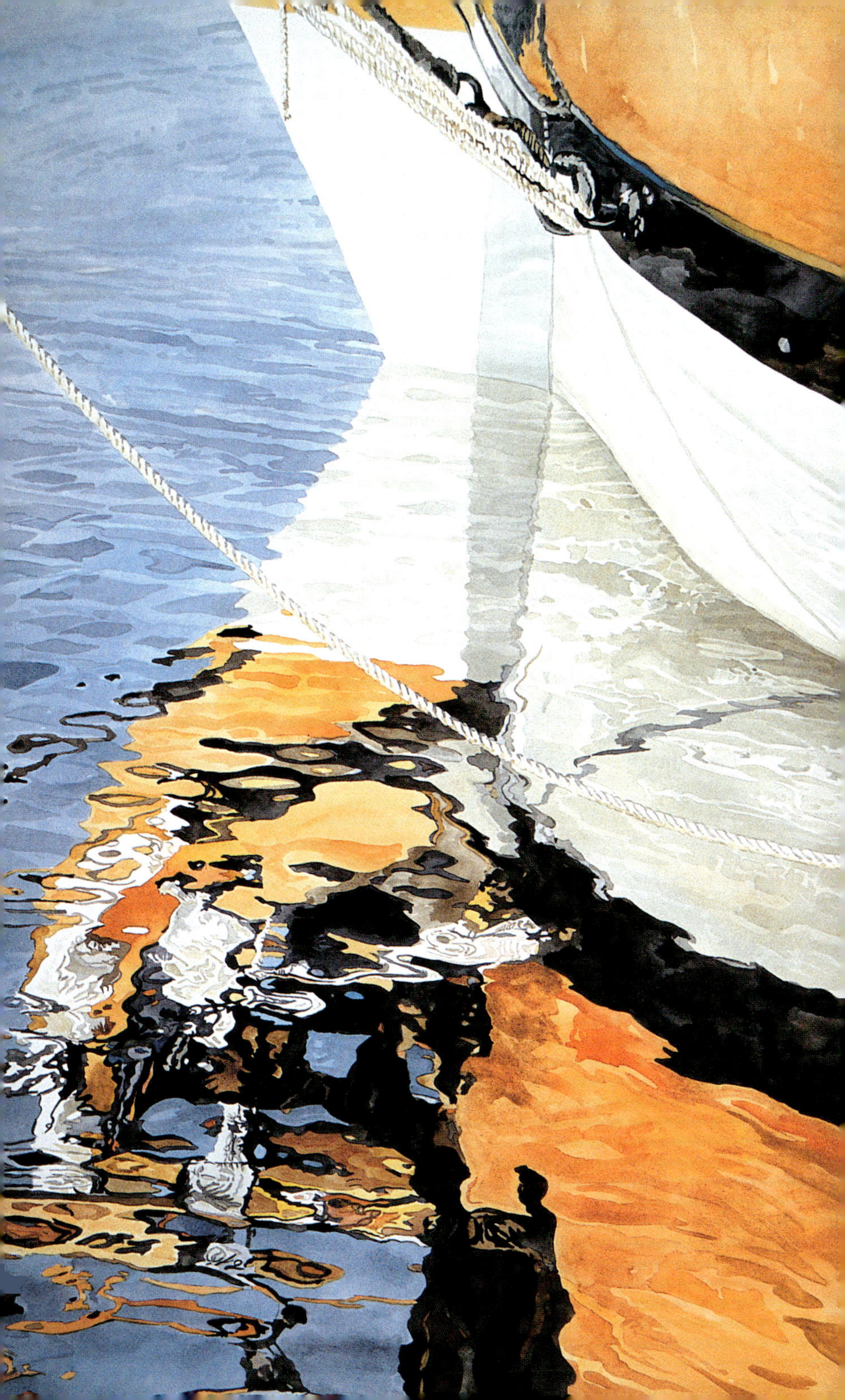

officer conveyed with all gravity.

"I am sure you have nothing to fear here. Clearer heads will prevail, and someone will get to the bottom of what *really* happened in Boston that night. The *Sultana* helped deliver those soldiers to that city, and none that we transported seem to fit the barbaric picture you have painted. They all struck me as conscientious soldiers, firm in their loyalty to the Crown."

The customs officer would not be swayed. He bid David Bruce good-day and took his armed guard with him back into the customs house. So Bruce and his men rowed the murder suspect and the madmen back to the schooner. The *Sultana* set sail that day down the James, arriving in Norfolk on March twenty-second, anchoring at noon in Hampton Road under hazy skies in five fathoms water by His Majesty's Ship *Boston*.

INGLIS LOGBOOK:

March 20, 1770 Working up the James River. Strong gales and cloudy weather. At 3pm came to anchor with the small bower in 3 fathoms water. Veered to 1/2 a cable Hog Island SSW 2 miles, the Custom house N 1 mile. Rec'd on board two mad men and two women to be deliv'd at Philadelphia.

It was a cloudy Sunday morning as the *Sultana* was moored in the Delaware River off Philadelphia. The crew all stood at attention on the quarter deck between the scuttle and the hatch—from which a steady wail issued. Inglis stood behind the binnacle, concluding their Sunday morning worship in a near shout to be heard over the din:

"Eternal Lord God, who alone spreadest out the heavens, and rulest the raging of the sea; who hast compassed the waters with bounds until day and night come to an end: Be pleased to receive into thy Almighty and most gracious protection the persons of us thy servants, and the Fleet in which we serve. Preserve us from the dangers of the sea, and from the violence of the enemy; that we may be a safeguard unto our most gracious Sovereign Lord, King George, and his Dominions, and a security for such as pass on the seas upon their lawful occasions; that the inhabitants of our Island may in peace and *quietness—*," Inglis inflected with a faint smirk, "— serve thee our God; and that we may return in safety to enjoy the blessings of the land, with the fruits of our labours, and with a thankful remembrance of thy mercies to praise and glorify thy holy Name; through Jesus Christ our Lord. Amen."

"Amen," echoed the crew in response as Inglis snapped shut his copy of the Book of Common Prayer. All were dismissed to their duties. During that day they took down the fore and main topmast, as well as the jib boom, and scraped them. The next watch got them up and rigged again. Then they scraped the main mast. Later that day Inglis sent Bruce to deliver their passengers from Hog Island.

Bruce and three other seamen led the motley crew of the criminal and the insane up from Market Street to the Mad House and then to the sheriff's offices. "I can't tell you how glad I am to be relieved of these people. Most of them were easy enough, but that mad woman, Morgan, was just about the end of us. I don't think she stopped her wailing during the entire journey up here. It got so bad yesterday that she just about unhinged our ship's clerk—and he wouldn't hurt a fly. I have never seen him in such an agitated state." Bruce's account illicited no response, so after the transaction was complete Bruce attempted to make conversation by asking, "So have you heard any more about the 'massacre' last month in Boston? When these people were placed in our care for transport, the custom officer there broke the news to me."

"Oh the 'massacre!'" the sheriff barked as he finished signing the paperwork for the transfer of Isleton into his custody. "If you ask me, conflict was inevitable. Look, as I understand it, roughly a quarter of the residents in Boston right now are soldiers. Not only do Bostonians resent 'foreign' troops in their city, the troops are so poorly paid that many are taking on part-time jobs—jobs needed by the colonists. What happened on the fifth was simply this: High tensions were hit by a snowball and all hell broke loose. A sentry on duty at the customs house had an argument with a local merchant and struck the man with the butt of his musket, which resulted in a crowd gathering and throwing things at the sentry—stones, oyster shells and the like. A larger crowd formed and soldiers came to the aid of the sentry. The mob taunted the soldiers, daring them to fire. Someone yelled, "Fire!" and the soldiers obliged. By the time order was restored, three colonists lay dead and two others mortally wounded."

"That certainly is a different story than I heard," commented Bruce, taken aback by both the sudden outpouring of opinions from the previously tight-lipped man and by the new revelations about the Boston conflict.

"Of course it is! That is because Samuel Adams and his

conspirators began calling it a 'massacre' in all of their propaganda. But the event certainly struck a chord in the heart of the city—a combined funeral held a few days later was said to have had 10,000 people in attendance."

"Well, I am very glad to hear all of this. What I heard originally troubled me greatly. I didn't want to believe servants of the Crown could be so rash and irresponsible," said Bruce with relief. Then he paused and reflected, "But I suppose none of us would want to be judged on how we might behave in a volatile situation like that. As I said, our mild ship's clerk turned rather violent with that screaming madwoman and... ah, well, it is good to know the King's men are faithfully carrying out their charge." Bruce continued to smile as inside he turned the news over and over in his mind.

INGLIS LOGBOOK:

April 1, 1770 Moor'd in Philadelphia Harbour Fresh breezes and cloudy weather. got down the topmast and scraped them. Sent the prisoners on shore to the jail.

The *Sultana* was stationed in Philadelphia until the twelfth of April—an important day for the small schooner, though none aboard would know why for some time. The following day they set off for the Chesapeake Bay. On the twenty-fourth she returned to her place in the company of HMS *Boston* as they sailed up the James River to Williamsburg. Both gave the Governor a seventeen-gun salute when he came to visit Sir Adams aboard the *Boston*.

Inglis, Bruce and the rest of the crew kept busy for the next couple months, patrolling all over that region including stops in Hampton Roads, York River, Lynnhaven River, Point Comfort, Cape Charles and Yorktown—often sailing alongside the *Boston*.

At the end of April, on the Elizabeth River near Point Comfort, twenty-six-year-old Irish sailor John Fitzgerald died during routine maintenance on the schooner. His senseless death, and the burial the following day, were recorded only in Bruce's log—Inglis's log took no notice of the loss of life.

On the second Friday in June, 1770, the *Sultana* fired two guns early in the morning to bring to the *Africa*, from Liverpool, bound to York River with salt. The inspection was carried out under unseasonably windy and rainy skies. The miserable conditions continued while the carpenter repaired the *Sultana's* small boat. Later that day the repaired craft took Bruce and several sailors over to the ship the *Lovely Friend* to inspect her. Once Bruce and his men boarded her, he began his well-worn litany:

"Captain, I am Master David Bruce of His Majesty's Schooner *Sultana* on board your ship by order of the King to enforce 15 Charles II, Chapter 7, An Act for the Encouragement of Trade. Under this Act—"

"We don't have any tea on board, Master Bruce, I assure you. But please feel free to search my ship," the *Lovely Friend's* captain interrupted.

"Errr—thank you for your willingness to support the Crown in this matter," Bruce said, losing his place. "But there are more items that we search for than just tea. We also look for glass, paint, oil, lead, paper—"

"Not any more," the *Lovely Friend's* captain interrupted again, cheerily. "I'd a' thought you would have heard by now. Back around the middle of April Prime Minister Lord North repealed all of the Townshend Revenue Act. Except for the tax on tea—but I imagine that that was kept on just to save face."

"I am afraid I did not follow—"

"Well, it was a bad bit of legislation, wasn't it? It didn't raise the money it had been want to—just raised a stink over here. But not to worry lad . . . you keep your job, if only to maintain

MADNESS

the principle of the right of parliament to tax the colonies."

"R-right then, we will just finish our search and get you back on your way, captain," Bruce answered in a bit of a fog. A ship from Boston would join up with the *Sultana* later that week to confirm the *Lovely Friend's* news. But in the meantime, the rain kept the mystified look on his face from being too apparent. Bruce, Inglis and the small crew of the schooner *Sultana* still had a job to do, but their justification for being in the American colonies was quickly shrinking.

INGLIS LOGBOOK:

June 8, 1770. In Chesapeake Bay Hard gales & squally with rain. At 1 pm weigh'd turning out of York River. Spoke with the Loving Friend merchant ship from England with goods, fired two guns to bring to a ship from England bound up the same river.

Washington

*I*NGLIS AND BRUCE WERE DECKED OUT IN their dress uniforms as they walked along the lane between formal gardens and hanging woods. Shadows were beginning to stretch across the bowling green, while at its far end, the lazy July sun bathed two stories of fine Georgian architecture in a warm and hazy glow. The house was actually made of pine but had been decorated to give the appearance of being crafted of stone. On the east side of the house, a lovely two-story piazza overlooked the Potomac River, while the servant's hall and other work houses were hidden from view by the beautiful rolling lawns.

Their host was a powerful member of the Virginia House of Burgesses, as well as being a colonel in the King's army, where he had served with distinction in the French and Indian War before creating this country gentleman's mansion. The lovely structure crowned five working farms, totaling nearly 8,000 acres, each with its own overseers, slaves, animals, buildings and equipment. The small party walked around the circular path in front of the commanding home, Bruce gawking a little—surprised to see something so lordly in the colonies.

"Welcome, gentlemen, to Mount Vernon," said George Washington as he greeted his guests, a slave ushering them in.

The two men offered curt bows, and Inglis said, "Lieutenant John Inglis of His Majesty's Schooner *Sultana* at your service, and this is my good friend Master David Bruce."

"A pleasure to meet you both," Washington said. "And may I present our other companion for dinner, Mr. John West. Please, come inside—my wife will join us shortly." And with that he drew them further into the entryway of the Washingtons' home. The central passage ran the width of the house and was set for entertaining guests. A zephyr wove through the passage and amongst the spindles of a prominent walnut staircase as the far doors were opened, providing a magnificent view of the Potomac.

"Pardon me, Colonel, but did you say that the name of your home is Mount Vernon? As in Admiral—?" queried Bruce.

"The very same. When these lands were originally

granted to my great-grandfather nearly one hundred years ago, it was known as Little Hunting Creek Plantation. My older half-brother, Lawrence, renamed it after Admiral Edward Vernon. Lawrence served under the Admiral in '41 as captain of the marines aboard Vernon's flagship."

"Wasn't Vernon's capture of Porto Bello, Panama, the first real battle begun with the affair of Jenkins' Ear?" asked Inglis.

"You know, I've heard about 'Jenkins' Ear' but, it being before my time, never understood the details of the conflict," Bruce interjected.

"In the spring of '31," John West said, "the captain of a Spanish coast guard sloop, the *San Antonio,* while trying to enforce trade laws that both sides were violating, stopped one of our merchant brigs—the *Rebecca.* Our man Captain Jenkins later told the House of Commons that the Spaniards had boarded his ship, accused them of smuggling, cut off his ear, pillaged the *Rebecca,* and then set her adrift. But I think it was the fact that his testimony was complete with his own pickled ear that gave his report such weight! So, Sir Robert Walpole reluctantly declared war on the Spanish in '39."

"And in spite of his victory and huge fame in England," George Washington finished, "poor Vernon later died after having been dismissed from the Royal Navy for disrespecting individuals on the Admiralty Board."

"And here we are, just over thirty years later, trying to stop smuggling again," mused Inglis.

"I can't quite agree that it is the same thing, Lieutenant," Washington commented tersely. Then turning to his wife he said, "Allow me to introduce you to my fine wife. Martha, we have the honor of hosting Lieutenant John Inglis of the schooner *Sultana* and her Master, David Bruce. The *Sultana* is at anchor near the estate of our good neighbor, Mr. Fairfax. And John's the brother of our friend, Samuel Inglis."

"We are honored, Ma'am," Inglis said as he and Bruce gave a slight bow, before adding, "We are anchored alongside the HMS *Boston* in Belvoir Reach. Sir Thomas Adams kindly extended your husband's invitation to us for dinner this evening."

"Yes, my husband has dined with the *Boston's* captain on several occasions, and we have had the pleasure of his company here as well. And your brother Samuel is a very fine man—we think highly of him," Martha said warmly.

"Mrs. Washington, your home is quite beautiful and seems to be in perfect harmony with its setting," David said.

"Thank you, Master Bruce, but I have to say that my husband must accept those kind words, for it was his vision that brought this to pass," replied Mrs. Washington. "When George inherited the property upon the death of his brother's widow almost a decade ago, it consisted of just four rooms, this central passage we are in now and three bedrooms on the second floor. Even before we were married he was

raising
the roof as well as
conducting a massive
redecorating campaign."

"George is ever the soldier, eh?" laughed West.

"If we are going to discuss my aesthetic battles here, then you must allow me to show off the best place in my house," said Washington as he ushered them into the front parlor, and Martha Washington excused herself. The summer sun poured in through two windows in the west wall and allowed a good light to take in the fully-paneled blue walls and Palladian door frames. Portraits adorned the walls and in the mantel—on the wall just opposite the entry—a carving of a griffin was to be found, bursting from a ducal coronet.

While admiring the room and giving the appropriate compliments, Bruce asked, "So Colonel, you and Mrs. Washington seem to be quite comfortably installed here. How long have you been married?"

"Eleven years," Washington answered. "Yet even in our first year together, I realized that I was fixed at this Seat with an agreeable Consort for life."

"Had you known each other long?" asked John.

"Not at all," laughed Washington. "We were engaged to be wed after having only spent time together twice. I've always been a bit shy around women. And if there were rewards given for unrequited love, I'd be a very rich man." Washington paused reflectively for a moment. "Ah, well, there is no reason to dwell on what was. Providence has afforded me an affectionate friend and worthy partner in Martha. We've never once had hateful words past between us, and I am very attached to her children from her first marriage." Washington looked out onto the bowling green before adding quietly and with a different look on his face, "I truly am quite fond of her."

"But what about you, Lieutenant Inglis?" Washington burst out as if he had just gotten his second wind. "What young lass is pining for you in Philadelphia?"

"Me? Ahh, none would have me. I would wager that none have been as unfortunate in affairs of the heart as I have. So I have sworn to only marry if I can find a woman ugly enough to frighten a horse!" laughed Inglis, not knowing he would do just that, less than seven years later. "Yet our handsome Master Bruce has a devoted following. Or there was at least that pretty young thing in Mousehole—Pender was her family name, wasn't it?" Inglis punched David in the arm to underscore the tease.

Bruce smiled and—suddenly inspecting his toes—replied, "That was a long time ago, and I am sure she has forgotten me by now!" John enjoyed needling David in this soft spot, and every time the topic was broached, Bruce had never been able to think up a verbal barb that he could counter that would cause equal embarrassment.

"Speaking of Philadelphia, I hear the famous Anglican revivalist George Whitefield arrived there in early May—have you seen him?" Washington asked as he poured drinks for him and his guests. "A powerful preacher they say. Thousands upon thousands flock to hear him. Even Benjamin Franklin is said to be an admirer."

"Thank you very much," John said as he accepted the glass. "No, we have been stationed here in the Chesapeake for some time. The last time we were in my 'home port' was this past March. It seems we just plod along on the King's business while all the important and exciting events of our day happen when we aren't around."

"Speaking of his Majesty, let us drink his honor. Long live King George," George said loudly as he lifted his glass. The others stuck their glasses to his and in unison echoed, "Long live King George!"

"It is good to hear you drink the King's health, Colonel," Inglis said after drinking to the Crown. "It had been my understanding that you had presented George Mason's resolutions to the Virginia House of Burgesses to ban British trade goods."

"Certainly I did," Washington bristled. "Mason is a neighbor and lifelong friend. But even if he weren't, I would have still proposed them. They were necessary. I also signed the newly revised Virginia Nonimportation Agreement that was sent to Governor Botetourt. And John and I were in Alexandria just yesterday, distributing copies of the agreement and gathering more signatures. We cannot stand by with hands folded as Parliament threatens to rob us of our political liberties—if trade can be taxed, then everything we have can be taxed. We could see a day when they taxed our property or food or clothing or anything! This kind of legislation would signal the end of self-government— which the Crown *guaranteed* in our colonial charter."

"Er—umm, yes. And certainly the Stamp Act took such liberties, but the Townshend Acts the *Sultana* are enforcing are external taxes and do not interfere with internal colonial governing. Besides, we are only searching for tea as of the twelfth of this past April," Bruce protested.

"Indeed, that was what I understood the rationale to be," Washington replied, unswayed. "The concerns of those in the colonies is that as British subjects under the English Constitution, we have rights to retain and grievances that need to be addressed through the system. It is my fear that regardless of how loyal we are to England and the English constitution, our lordly Masters in Great Britain will be satisfied with nothing less than the deprivation of American freedom. It was clear to me that something should be done to avert the stroke and maintain the liberty which we have derived from our ancestors." Then he redirected their conversation by saying, "It looks like dinner is ready, gentlemen. Let us see what culinary delights await us."

The dinner party walked to the other room and relief washed over Bruce at not having to defend his assertion in any further debate with their host. But with that wave of emotion came an undertow of doubt. If his service to the Crown was the right thing to do, why was he so defensive? And how could someone who had served the King so famously in the late war support this unloyal position? And why did Washington's arguments sound so sane to him?

The conversation turned to mutual friends and anecdotes from on deck, with the evening ending cool and clear. Inglis and Bruce reluctantly returned to the *Sultana* and continued to work with the *Boston* in that region.

Toward the middle of August the *Sultana* set sail from Cape Henry on the Chesapeake Bay to Halifax Harbor in Nova Scotia for re-fitting and re-provisioning, as she had done the year before. Poseidon was unkind to the little schooner as she sailed to Nova Scotia, taking from her a main topsail yard, the log line, the lead line, the flying jib stay and, more seriously, twenty-eight-year-old John Smith—the ship's original gunner's mate.

Under the fine care of Jim Wagner, Halifax's chief shipwright, the *Sultana* was cleaned out, the hull painted, the deck caulked, new rigging put up and five of the cannons repaired. The crew was overhauled as well, with Commodore Hood ordering the discharge of three men and Andrew McKenzie being transferred from HMS *Romney*.

On the sixth of September the *Sultana* set sail for Boston.

Peace

*V*IPER, A SLOOP IN THE SERVICE OF THE Crown, along with the HMS *Rose* were in Boston Harbor when the refitted *Sultana* arrived from Halifax on the eleventh of September. But as the *Sultana* dropped anchor, there was no warm homecoming some might expect for a schooner that had been built here in Benjamin Hallowell's Boston shipyard only three years earlier. No, she was now returning as part of the despised Royal Navy fleet in America, and only six short months after the Boston Massacre—an event whose wake would soon carry the Royal Navy's North American headquarters with it down from Halifax to Boston. Also, Boston still held onto its Nonimportation Agreement, even if New York and

Philadelphia had returned to normal trade relations with Britain with the repeal of the majority of the Townshend Acts.

INGLIS LOGBOOK:

September 11, 1770. Moderate breezes and clear weather, saw Cape Ann bearing WNW 5 leagues, handed the topsails, see the lights of Boston bearing WSW 6 leagues, came to anchor in Boston Harbour in 16 fathoms water with the anchor and hawser, found riding here His Majesty's Ship Rose and Viper sloop.

Yet for all the animosity that Boston held for the *Sultana* and her kin, the ships only garnered the amount of attention one absent-mindedly gives to a fly while swatting it away. This was because the whole city was buzzing with excitement over the visit of the famous preacher George Whitefield.

Born in 1714, Whitefield was an Oxford graduate, a member of a religious group the Wesley brothers made famous, called the Holy Club, and chaplain to the Countess of Huntington. He was in Boston as part of his seventh evangelistic preaching tour of the colonies. George Whitefield had arrived in the city on the fifteenth of August while the *Sultana* was sailing in the Atlantic off Nantucket on

Peace

its way to Halifax, Nova Scotia. For three days in September he had been too ill to preach, but as soon as he could be out of bed, he was back preaching. Thousands upon thousands would come from all parts of Boston to hear this famous man preach:

" . . . says Jeremiah, *'They have healed also the hurt of the daughter of my people slightly, saying, Peace, peace, when there is no peace.'* The prophet, in the name of God, had been denouncing war against the people, he had been telling them that their house should be left desolate, and that the Lord would certainly visit the land with war."

On the day following their arrival, David Bruce joined the ship's clerk William Dearl as he came into town with some of the crew to obtain supplies in the *Sultana's* never-ending task of staying stocked. "Run, geese!" yelled a scruffy little boy amongst a group of children playing "Fox and Geese" as Bruce and Dearl walked by on their way to buy rum.

"Well, Will, you have been serving on the *Sultana* for over two years now. Do you miss the HMS *Achilles?*"

Dearl coughed a short laugh and said, "You can't really compare them, can you? A sixty-gun ship with four hundred and twenty men aboard versus the fleet's smallest schooner—basically a fifty-foot floating thimble! I'd say apples and oranges have more in common than the *Achilles* and the *Sultana*."

"Now, Will, we have enough problems with merchant ships teasing us because of our size and flying pendants to insult us. I expected a little more kindness from one of our own," Bruce said with a good-natured smirk.

"Well, one thing that was better on the *Achilles* was that it was easier to find people willing to do their job. Most times an order is given on the *Sultana*, it seems like the seaman is walking through mud to accomplish it. Though there are exceptions—Jurd was awfully excited to go to the bakery for us," commented Dearl.

"Yes, it seems that the baker has a daughter that John is taken with. I told him that whenever we are in Boston I would send him with you for provisions. Besides, I trust him not to run off at the first chance he gets ashore—a trait that is sadly lacking in most of our crew."

The two officers of the *Sultana* rounded the corner and found themselves unexpectedly in the middle of a throng of Boston residents with a booming voice soaring over their heads.

"Excuse me," Bruce asked one of the individuals standing near him, "What is going on here?"

"Shhh! I'm trying to listen to the Reverend Whitefield,"

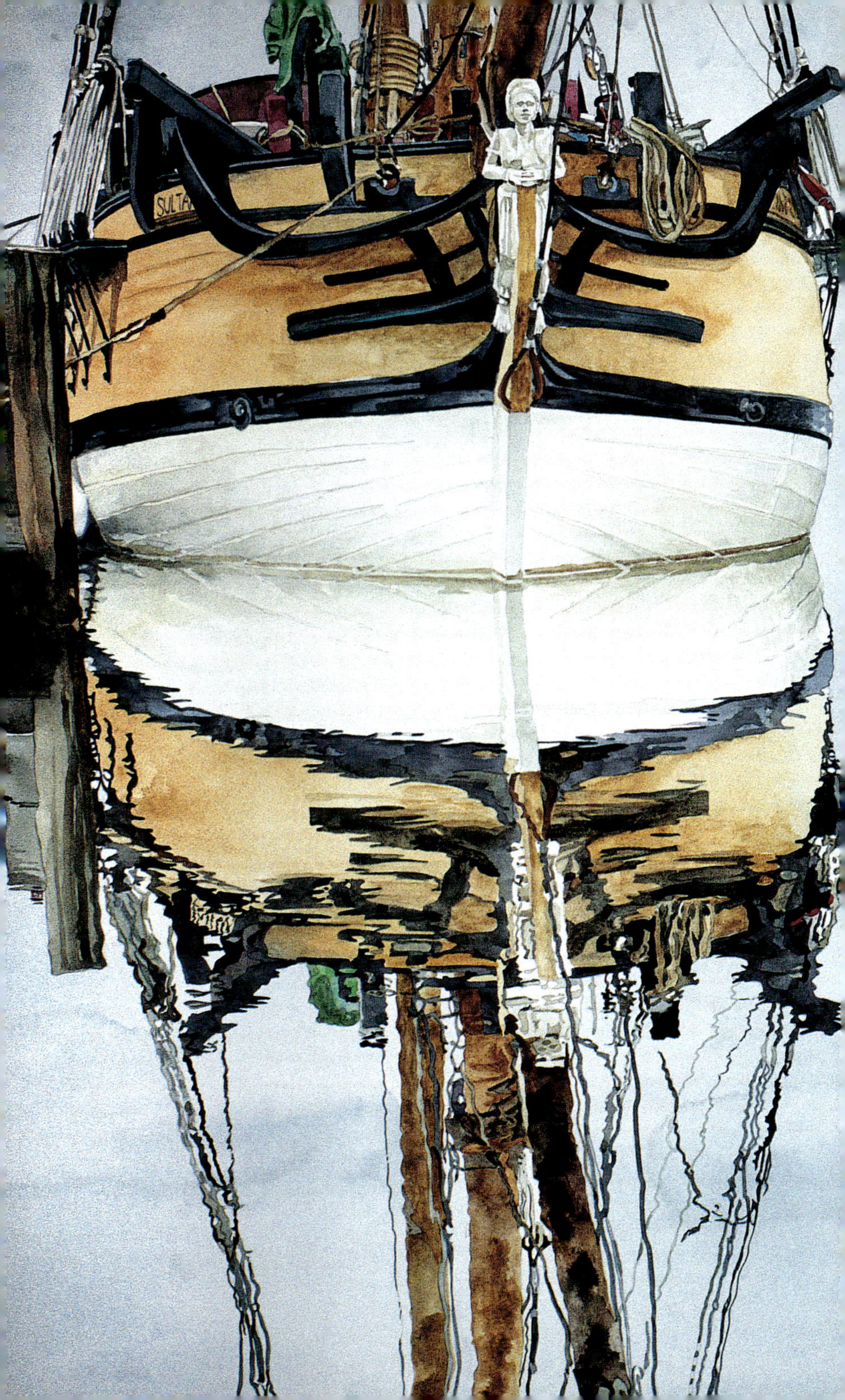

the man whispered crossly.

They heard the preacher proclaim, "It is a matter, therefore, of great importance, my dear hearers, to know whether we may speak peace to *our* hearts. We are all desirous of peace; peace is an unspeakable blessing; how can we live without peace? And, therefore, people from time to time must be taught how far they must go, and what must be wrought in them, before they can speak peace to their hearts."

"*We* won't have any peace from the crew if we don't get those barrels of rum we are needing," Dearl whispered with a tug and a wink to Bruce. Bruce nodded, and they ducked down an alley to try and circumvent the crowds.

Dearl and Bruce found their way to the seller of spirits but had to look around to find the short proprietor with a large bushy beard back among all the barrels. He was sweating hard and was nearly as wide as he was tall, making him seem a twin to the barrels he was selling.

"How can I help you, gentlemen?" he asked as he mopped his brow. "I didn't think I would be seeing much business while the Reverend was preaching, or I would have been out in the front of the warehouse by my desk."

"His Majesty can't have his sailors listening to sermons when there are smugglers to catch," joked Bruce.

"I need to purchase thirty barrels of rum from you for the schooner *Sultana*," Dearl said. "Here are vouchers that you can redeem with London for your payment."

"Quite fine, young sirs. I have dealt with the British Admiralty many times," the rum merchant said. "I suppose you will want to carry those back to the ship yourselves?" he bantered. "No? then I must ask you allow me some time for my hands to return from 'church' with Whitefield, and then I will have them bring a wagon around to the docks for you."

"That will be good. We have several other stops to make and will meet them there later. Thank you for your help, sir," William Dearl said, and both he and Bruce bowed slightly and left the building.

"I have to go order firewood," Dearl said. "Do you want to go hear Boston's famous guest, and I will meet you back at the baker's? I imagine we will both be needed to pry Mr. Jurd away from his lass."

Bruce laughed in agreement and added, "Perhaps we will need to preach to him that 'Man shall not live by bread alone'," Dearl guffawed, and they parted company. David Bruce walked towards the epicenter of city life that day—watching his steps to avoid the small reoccurring monuments to horse life in the cobbled streets as well as the kitchen garbage that would occasionally fly from windows—while following the strong, compelling voice:

"... before you can speak peace to your hearts, you must not only be troubled for the sins of your life, the sin of your nature, but likewise for the sins of your best duties and performances. As Adam and Eve hid themselves among the trees of the garden, and sewed fig leaves together to cover their nakedness, so the poor sinner, when awakened, flies to his duties and to his performances, to hide himself from God, and goes to patch up a righteousness of his own. There must be a deep conviction before you can be brought out of your self-righteousness; it is the last idol taken out of our heart. The pride of our heart will not let us submit to the righteousness of Jesus Christ. Can you now say from your heart, *Lord, thou mayst justly damn me for the best duties that ever I did perform?* If you are not thus brought out of self, you may speak peace to yourselves, but yet there is no peace."

Bruce caught his breath and stopped walking for half a beat of his heart as the preacher's words struck him to the marrow: *damn me for the best duties that ever I did perform.* Could that be true? Could his submission and obedience to the King be a damning service?

The Master of the *Sultana* eventually arrived back at the spot they had first encountered the impromptu congregation. David wended his way through the outer fringes of the entirely silent crowd, to stand at a point as close to the preacher as he could without shoving others out of the way. Whitefield had a loud and clear voice, and articulated his words and sentences so perfectly, that he might be heard and understood at a great distance. At a sermon preached in Philadelphia, Benjamin Franklin had once calculated that Whitefield was heard by more than thirty thousand people.

The Boston crowd was not that vast, but it was much larger than Bruce had imagined it would be at first. This meant that he was still blocks away from the podium that had been erected for Whitefield, but he could see him well and hear him clearly promulgate, ". . . I am persuaded the devil believes more of the Bible than most of us do. He believes the divinity of Jesus Christ; he believes and trembles, and that is more than thousands amongst us do. My friends, we mistake a historical faith for a true faith, wrought in the heart by the Spirit of God. You fancy you believe, because you believe there is such a book as we call the Bible—because you go to church; all this you may do, and have no true faith in Christ. Merely to believe there was such a person as Christ, merely to believe there is a book called the Bible, will do you no good, more than to believe there was such a man as Caesar or Alexander the Great."

David Bruce found himself quite enraptured by the delivery and content of the Reverend: Was his faith true or just historical? If his faith in Christ was an empty acceptance of fact, what did that say about his fealty to the Crown? Was his loyalty a matter of just doing what he was told instead of doing what was right? And with a start he shook his head, as he suddenly realized he had lost all sense of time. He did not want to be late meeting back up with the schooner's clerk. So he zigzagged as quickly as he could out of the crowd and made for the baker's.

He soon found able-bodied seaman John Jurd by a wheelbarrow filled to overflowing with bread. Jurd was leaning slightly against the side of the building, talking to a young woman who stood halfway inside the door leading into the bakery, with a basket in her hand.

"Busy at work for His Majesty King George, Mr. Jurd?" Bruce called out as he approached.

John nearly fell over as he spun and quickly recovered into a salute before stammering, "Yes, sir—no, sir—err, may I introduce you to our baker's daughter, sir?

"I would be delighted if you would do me that honor," Bruce smiled.

"Master Bruce, this is Miss Annie Donovan—Miss Donovan, this is Master David Bruce of the H. M. Schooner *Sultana*," John Jurd said, almost completely recovered from a furiously red face by now.

The master and the young lady greeted one another, Bruce bowing as the lady curtsied, her large green-flecked eyes hid briefly by her bonnet. Honey-brown curls escaped around her heart-shaped face and full lips broke into a half smile as she spoke, "Master Bruce, it is a pleasure to make your aquaintance. John has spoken highly of your service together and of your fair managing of the crew."

"Thank you. It has been an honor to serve with John as well. He is loyal, dependable and knows his trade well. I only wish his job were easier. But day after day resistance to our work gets stronger—no one seems to believe that maintaining peace and prosperity should be paid for."

"Honestly, Master Bruce, most common folk I know give little thought to the taxes you enforce."

"Ah, I think—" Bruce began, but Miss Donovan plowed on, not noticing his reply.

"What concerns us are the attempts that keep being made to land a bishop on our shores. The Society for Propagating the Gospel in Foreign Parts is busy trying to bring this about, even though such an action would require an act of Parliament, and so violate the laws of God embodied in our colonial charters with the Crown." Annie was moved to passion as she spoke, and her skin flushed, making the stray flour about her person more visible. "I am sure you know that during the Stamp Act those in the Society were overly loyal to England and opposed all actions to rid us of the tax!"

"As to that—" Bruce interjected.

"Many fear that asking for bishops is all part of a great plot to deliver the Puritan colonies back into the hands of king and bishops."

"Well, I am sure—" Jurd started to say, while torn between admiration and dying of sheer embarrassment.

"A colonial bishop would be just another agent of British tyranny—spiritual tyranny. And if we lose our spiritual liberties, can our political liberties be far behind?" Annie asked rhetorically.

"I can't imagine *that* ever—" Bruce threw in.

"If Parliament can create dioceses and appoint bishops, nothing could hinder them from forbidding marriages carried out by dissenting ministers or even forbidding dissent—perhaps requiring such spiritual criminals to forfeit life and property!"

Bruce was saved from further verbal battle on the seas of religious and political life by the arrival of William Dearl. "Ah, Will, I believe you've met the ardent daughter of our baker? Good. Well, we must be off—I am sure that rum has arrived at the dock by now."

The three sailors bid farewell to the baker's daughter and walked back to the docks as she returned to managing the shop. As they passed by the center of town, powerful words rode on the breeze to them, declaring:

"Would you have peace with God? Away, then, to God through Jesus Christ, Who has purchased peace; the Lord Jesus has shed His heart's blood for this. He died for this; He rose again for this; He ascended into the highest heaven, and is now interceding at the right hand of God. Perhaps you think there will be no peace for you. Why so? Because you are sinners? Yet there is peace for you. Pray, what did Jesus Christ say of his disciples, when He came to them the first day of the week? He showed them His hands and His side, and said, 'Peace be unto you.'"

Peace be unto you? As Master David Bruce climbed into the cutter, he reflected on the preacher's words again. What with taxes, bishops and people uttering the word "Crown" as if it were a curse, it seemed to Bruce as if this place were the last place anyone could find peace.

After spending nearly two weeks in Boston Harbor conducting several small ships entering the harbor, the *Sultana* set sail for Halifax, joining up with the *Boston* on the 24th. She was carrying orders from the Lords of the Admiralty to Commodore Hood, instructing him, in the wake of March fifth's clash, to make the city of Boston the new headquarters of the North Atlantic Station. The *Sultana* spent just over a week in Hampton Road before having to turn right around to arrive on November third in Rhode Island. Commodore Gambier had been informed in a letter dated August 21, 1770, of a prodigious illegal shipment—four hundred large chests of tea were said to be on their way in two sloops from Holland, hidden in rice barrels. The *Sultana* was ordered to block off New York from the smugglers by sailing back and forth between Montauk Point and Fishers Island. Two weeks were then spent on a wild goose chase, based on intelligence that was delivered too late to be of value. The shipment had been unloaded before the trap was even set.

INGLIS LOGBOOK:

November 23, 1770. Fishers Island ENE 4 miles. Cloudy & Hazy thick weather. At 11 am Boarded the Polly Sloop Bound to Dartmouth with Ballast & Some Provisions & the Greyhound Sloop with wood to Nantucket Island. At 2 pm aired the sails. The people Employed Looking out for the two Sloops which were to Come From Amsterdam with Contraband Goods.

The *Sultana* stayed in the Rhode Island waters for most of the winter—but not all on board stayed with her. On the second of December James Gore deserted after having been recently flogged with twenty-four lashes from the cat's tail for mutinous behavior. At this time many men would seek to find peace from their labors aboard the schooner by running off. Some, like Gore, were successful—and some were not.

Polly

Thomas Roberts had been pressed into the crew of the *Sultana* two months previous and had almost immediately escaped. Bruce and several of the *Sultana's* finest now stood on board a merchant ship in Newport, looking right at him. "Upon my word, the prodigal returns," Bruce said with a mirthless laugh.

The twenty-three-year-old Welsh sailor turned pale and with clenched fists declared, "I am not returning to that tub, Master Bruce. The *Sultana* is a miserable hole in the water. I want to work on a ship that might afford me a decent life—serving 'Farmer George' is going to get me a big sack of nothing! Why, if you ask me—"

"Jurd, Grant—grab our good friend Mr. Roberts." Bruce's

order interrupted the renegade sailor's tirade. John and Charles went to obey just as another young sailor from the merchant ship stepped in the way.

"Out of the way, boy," Charles Grant said as he knocked aside Roberts' defender and grabbed an arm as the wayward seaman began to scramble backwards. Jurd quickly grabbed the other arm as the deserter began to struggle and flail about, arching his back and falling to the deck. Roberts set loose a torrent of profanity as he was dragged away. Many murmurs and whispered complaints arose from the crew, but no one, for fear of being pressed, came to his aid.

The slate gray January sky slowly darkened, and flakes began to swirl as the merchant ship moved off towards shore and Thomas Roberts was returned to his shipmates aboard the *Sultana*. It seemed like no time at all before Piddle the midshipman was calling for the *Sultana's* captain.

"Lieutenant Inglis—sir, it looks like we may have a situation brewing on shore."

Inglis turned to see what Piddle was pointing at, frowned, calmly leaned over the quarter deck hatch and said, "Mr. Bruce, would you care to join me on the poop deck?"

Bruce launched himself up the ladder and was buttoning his overcoat against the cold as he emerged from the quarter deck hatch. "Yes, Lieutenant?"

Bruce stood with Inglis and Piddle leeward of the large flag flying off the aft railing. The wind kicked up, and the shoreline was intermittently obscured as the ship's colors cracked and twisted. Each time the flag passed before their field of vision and retreated, more angry colonists seemed to appear out of thin air.

Angry screams drifted across the water, such as: "Give us back Tom!" "Go home to your Royal Buttonmaker and leave us alone!" "We'll burn you to the waterline!" "Thieving-no-good-leeches!" "Give back Roberts!" "Spanish guarda-costas!" "Cut her lines!" and the like.

"It appears that news of our prodigal's return has reached the good people of Newport," Bruce smiled ruefully, as those along the shore got into small boats and took out their oars.

"I do believe they intend to board us," Inglis commented with mock indifference. Turning around to the rest of the ship, he yelled, "Clear for action! Mr. Nichollson, please place all eight swivel guns aft here and load with grapeshot. You will fire on my command. Master Bruce, please have Piddle join you in visiting the magazine so we can properly arm the crew." The deck of the *Sultana* became a frenzied ant hill of activity as each man went to his assigned task.

Bruce and Piddle had just returned to deck with armfulls of pistols when Inglis directed those hands at the cannons, "Aim for the water just ahead of them, if you please," and yelled, "FIRE!"

The entire aft of the *Sultana* was filled with a cacophony of sound and thick smoke. As the air cleared, Bruce and

Piddle began to pass out arms. Angry shouts burst out from the small boats and the shoreline mob, as Bruce turned to see the would-be boarders turn and row in a muddle, some toward shore, some into each other, and a few brave souls on toward the *Sultana*.

"Reload," ordered Inglis. But the order to fire was never repeated, as the heavens themselves joined the fray. Hard gales and snow exploded from the dark sky, obscuring everyone's vision. As the first wave of bad weather ebbed, Bruce looked to see the boats all turning back and the rioters on the shore running for cover. The *Sultana* relaxed, and they set sail to put some distance between them and the shore.

BRUCE LOGBOOK:

Monday 21 Calms WSW WbS Great Island NE 1 mile Light breezes & calms. At 11 am unmoored, hove short, weighed & came to sail. The boat returned from town at noon. Came to anchor with the best bower in 3 1/2 fathoms. Veered to 1/2 cable the fort on Great Island NE 1 mile. The people employed in clearing the decks and loading all the swivels & small arms because the people of Newport threatened to board us & cut us off & to burn the schooner for taking Thomas Roberts out of a snow bound to Antigua which he had run from the schooner 2 months before.

Wednesday 23 NNE North NBW Hard gales & snow with strong frost. At 8am let go the small bower anchor, veered to 1/3 cable on the best bower & 1/2 cable on the small. At 9am the Polly schooner made the signal of distress. Sent the boat to her assistance with 10 men. The people got her off the rocks & carried her into Rhode Island Harbor & anchored her in safety. At noon the boat returned from the Polly. The people employed variously.

No desertions were recorded over those first two bitterly cold months in 1771. Quite the contrary, deserters from the

Salisbury and *Senegal* were in fact *recovered* during this time. Hard gales and frost ripped across the small schooner, requiring the crew to be diligent in their labors, breaking ice from the hull and shoveling the deck to keep it clear of snow. The wicked winter took its toll on the *Sultana,* but it also took its pound of flesh—Midshipman William Piddle fell into poor health and was sent ashore to recover in more hospitable environs.

Except for able-bodied seaman Robert Whaley getting twenty-four lashes for stealing, the remainder of the winter passed without incident. Basic repairs to the ship, collecting firewood and spinning yarn kept them from being completely frozen with the monotony of life aboard the *Sultana* through the winter.

In March, the ship and her crew began to thaw out as they sailed, along with a not-quite-cured midshipman, to New York for new orders. Once in New York Harbor, the *Sultana* was towed to shore with the ship's cutter for careening. Once ashore, the *Sultana* was hove down using a winch and a cable that was attached high up on the mast of the ship. The other end wound around something similar to the *Sultana's* windlass. The men walked around it like they were raising an anchor, but instead they were pulling the ship down to them. Once on her side, the careening of the *Sultana* consisted of removing barnacles and sea worms. These had to be scraped off before applying a coat of turpentine and brimstone. After repairs, the *Sultana* received orders to sail back to Rhode Island to retrieve revenues that had been collected by the Newport customs house and then take them on to Boston.

The *Sultana* and her crew arrived in Rhode Island on the twelfth of April under cloudy skies. Bitter gales filled the sails of the *Sultana* as she changed tack to head southeast to clear the southern end of Goat Island on her approach to Newport. *Sultana* arrived in the harbor and anchored at four in the afternoon, and by that time a great deal of activity had sprung up around the customs house.

Bruce raised a spyglass to his eye and scanned the shore. "Curtis, lad . . . go down and tell the Lieutenant I respectfully request his company on deck." The young cabin boy was gone in a flash and returned at the heels of Inglis.

"What is the trouble, Master Bruce?"

David handed the spyglass to Inglis. The noise of the disturbance had reached them, already making it nearly unnecessary to view it through the glass. "I imagine that our arrival in Newport is not quite a welcomed event. That mob looks worse than the one that tried to take Roberts back in January."

"Hmmm . . . I hadn't thought picking up a chest of the King's property would prove so challenging," Inglis said as he looked through the small telescope. "Oh no—those half-wits! It looks like they have taken the Collector and beaten him." Everyone on deck stiffened as the schooner gently rocked up and down on the lazy swell of the harbor. "Master Bruce—fill the cutter with as many men as you can. Arm yourself to the teeth. We must stop this anarchy!"

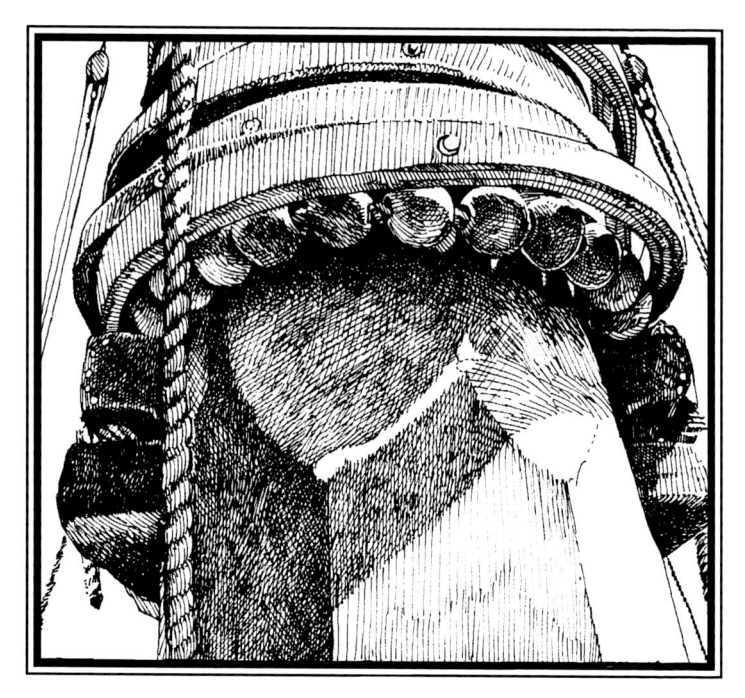

"Yes, sir," Bruce replied as his eyes met Inglis's steely gaze. Both men knew what was expected of them, and both set off to follow those divergent paths of service to the Crown. "Nichollson, Lee and Whaley—go to the magazine and empty it of enough powder horns, flintlocks, muskets, swords and pistols for fourteen of us. I know there aren't enough pistols for us each to have two, but bring all that are there."

"Aye aye," the three men chimed.

"Brenson, Grant and Burrell, you take the weapons from

them as they hand them up and stow them on the cutter. McKenzie, bring the cutter around. Mr. Piddle, you will be joining us—please go below and instruct Mr. Jennison, Robert, Henry, Tom, John and George to come with us as well." With amazing speed each man set about his task, and it wasn't long before they were climbing into the small boat.

Abram Lee was at the tiller, Bruce and Abram in the bow, and Walter Burrell, Robert Whaley, Henry Roach and Thomas Ritchie each at an oar. They shoved off and began into shore where the crowd was growing larger and louder. Lit torches had appeared.

The *Sultana's* men scrambled out of the ship's boat and arranged themselves to confront the mob. They were sailors, not soldiers, so it would be a stretch to say they "marched" on the customs house to face the rioters, but they did proceed in an orderly fashion. "Take aim," Bruce ordered, then added quietly, "but no one shoot unless I tell them to. We don't want the *Sultana* responsible for a 'Boston massacre' here."

"We'll not have the King squeezing our livelihood from us!" one man yelled.

"We are here to support and protect the servant of the Crown you are most heinously abusing," David Bruce yelled in response.

"Stand back, you tars—we are just taking our rightful monies. This is no concern of yours!" retorted another from the crowd.

"The monies in this building are the King's Property, forfeited by smugglers—" began Bruce, only to be drowned out by screams and curses.

"Steady men—hold your fire," Bruce instructed his crew, then fired his pistol into the air. "You must all disperse, in the name of the King!"

The blast from the pistol made several of the rioters jump back. In the brief silence after the shot, muskets were cocked among the *Sultana's* crew. Then as with one mind the mob began to break up and run off, but not before giving the customs officer a few more blows and throwing a fragment of brick at the sailors.

The brick struck a grazing blow to the skull of the boatswain Abram Lee, who stumbled to the ground. "Piddle, see to the customs officer," yelled Bruce as he hurried over to help Lee.

Bruce inspected the older sailor quickly and said, "It looks like you'll need a little care from Mr. Haliburton—but I've seen worse. Jurd, Roach . . . please help Mr. Lee. Piddle, how much abuse did that mob inflict on that fellow?"

The midshipman began to gingerly lift the customs officer while Burrell and Ritchie formed a rough guard by the door to the customs house. "I think he'll be all right, sir."

"Thank you—I am most grateful for your assistance," the customs officer said.

"How do you account for such anarchy, sir? This area has

had its struggles...but this is unprecedented," Piddle remarked as he helped the customs officer up into a seated position.

"Sadly, this sort of behavior is not entirely unexpected. Just last week the *Polly* arrived in Newport with illegal cargo," the bloodied officer recounted. "The tidesman who boarded her and made the discovery was thanked for doing his duty to the Crown with a blow to the back of his skull!"

"He lost consciousness," he continued. "Then the villains treated him in a most inhuman fashion. After that they violently dragged him into the main street to leave him to rot."

"These colonists are animals," snarled Nichollson, the *Sultana's* gunner.

"That is not the entirety of it! After the hooligans unloaded the *Polly*, they tarred and feathered a man they suspected of being an informer against them. These people have shown continual animosity towards all those involved with customs. There is no telling how far they will go. I hate to think what might have happened today if you had not arrived when you did." With those words spoken, the servant of the Crown promptly fainted from his injuries.

The adrenaline rush from the melee with the rioters was beginning to wane in Bruce, only to be replaced by a simmering anger as the customs officer's words sunk in. There was no peace here in these colonies! To think, he had entertained the notion that his submission and obedience to the King might be a damning service. Now the challenging words of the preacher inverted into a rallying cry—to *not* serve the King in the face of this anarchy would be the damning service!

INGLIS LOGBOOK:

April 12, 1771. Anchored in Newport Harbor. Hard gales and cloudy weather. At 4 pm Manned and armed the Boat to go on Shore to Assist the Collector of His Majesty's Customs at Rhode Island. He Seized a Brig that was running their Cargo, & the Mob gathered & beat him, & threatened to pull down the Custom house & Seize on the King's property, sent the pilot on shore

At seven the following Tuesday morning, the ship's boat was manned, armed and sent to shore to retrieve the money. The King's chest was taken on board the *Sultana* for transport to Boston, containing collected duties of £600 in sterling silver. Mercifully, the entire transaction was made without event. The pilot, Mr. Pease, also returned to the *Sultana,* and they set sail for Boston on the following day.

Inglis Logbook

April 19, 1771 Going up Boston Bay Strong breezes and clear weather. At 7 pm Cape Cod WbS 2 leagues. Sounded 31 fathoms. Set the square sail & topsail. At 10 came to anchor with the small bower in 2 1/2 fathoms water, Boston Long Wharf WNW 2 cables length. Found here His Majesty's Ship Salisbury & Viper sloop. Saluted Commodore Gambier with 13 1/2 pounders.

On Saturday, amidst strong gales and rain, the ship's boat was sent to shore with the King's money and Midshipman Piddle. They hoped that time ashore would provide a full recovery from the illness that dogged him. Later the same day they pressed two men out of a Nantucket sloop. Deserters that the *Sultana* had recovered in Newport were returned to the *Salisbury* for punishment, and the *Salisbury* helped restock the *Sultana* with new eating bowls and platters, as well as fresh slops. Dearl requisitioned fresh beef, bread, pork, butter and cheese for the schooner. And, of course, able-bodied seaman John Jurd was given the job of retrieving the bread.

One week later Commodore Gambier ordered the

schooner *Sultana* to patrol the area around Sandy Hook, and over the next two and a half months they searched over eighty vessels. No smugglers were found, even with the occasional aid of the *Deal Castle* and the *Mercury*. But fruitless searches did not squelch David Bruce's renewed zeal for their duties. The cruel winter was over, but any softening to the colonists' plight had frozen in the heart of the *Sultana's* master. He was committed to hunting down every one of their ships and squashing their illegal trade. Bruce was now completely mystified how he ever could have found any legitimacy in the fickle behavior of those disloyal dullards.

King George

"Sail off the port bow!"

Fourteen-year-old Robert Beck bellowed news of his sighting from up in the rigging. He had been indentured into naval life aboard the *Sultana* for the payment of his father's debts. Charles Grant served as Beck's "sea-daddy" and had taught him all he knew about knotting and splicing and generally how to get along. Though initially sullen and reclusive, now, just a month and three days later, the New Yorker had embraced life at sea.

"Well sighted, Mr. Beck," Master Bruce yelled back encouragingly. "Mr. Roberts, please give chase. We shall see what that merchant ship is hiding in her belly. I will inform Lieutenant Inglis."

Peeking his head into the Lieutenant's cabin, Bruce said, "John, young Robert just sighted a ship, and we're giving chase."

"Thank you, David," Inglis said, looking up from the logs. "Perhaps she will be a great golden prize ship, and we can retire from the Service and finally get to leave these perfidious colonies."

"Wouldn't that be grand? But at this rate Hell will freeze over before we're allowed to leave the colonies," Bruce rejoined.

Upon returning to deck, Bruce took a look through a telescope at their quarry and was dispirited to learn that it wasn't a potential prize. "It's just the *Rose*," Bruce called down to the Lieutenant through the grated hatch. The twenty-gun HMS *Rose* had been launched fourteen years earlier and had fought in the French and Indian War. It was now under the command of Captain Caldwell. Once the *Sultana* was alongside, Caldwell ordered her to accompany him to the Delaware Colony's town of New Castle—a major shipping area that had a well-earned reputation for corruption.

On Thursday, the eighteenth of July, the *Sultana* came to anchor in New Castle, the HMS *Rose* having already anchored in the harbor. Inglis asked Dearl to add to his regular restocking the hiring of two coopers. During the *Sultana's* stay in that port these men came aboard to repair its broken and leaky casks.

The next day, His Majesty's Schooner *Gaspee* sailed into New Castle. The *Gaspee* was famous for the amount of prize money she had earned—one thousand pounds in one seizure alone, less than a year ago in the Delaware River. The *Gaspee* was also infamous for her haughty, insolent and intolerable Scottish Lieutenant William Dudingston. Dudingston had taken command of the *Gaspee* in September of 1768, just after she had been refitted to become a twin-masted schooner.

Master Bruce climbed up onto the deck of the *Gaspee* several days later and saluted. "Master David Bruce of His Majesty's Schooner *Sultana,* sir. I am here to come and help evaluate your anchor line."

"Welcome Master Bruce—but really this is unnecessary. Even a lubberly fool of a colonist could tell it needs to be replaced," Lieutenant William Dudingston said in greeting to David Bruce.

"Truly I do not know sir, I am here on Captain Keeler's order," Bruce answered with a mildly defensive tone.

"Well, go on then . . . I dare say you don't need me to show you around. The *Gaspee* and the *Sultana* are nearly identical twins. Though not identical in *prize money,* I dare say," said Dudingston as he laughed superciliously.

"Mmmm . . . as you say, sir," replied Bruce. "I'll just be about it now, if that is fine with you, sir?"

"Of course, of course. Stop in my cabin when you are done to report the inevitable conclusion to your investigation." The lieutenant turned and slid down the ladder through the quarter deck hatch.

Walking along the deck of the *Gaspee* was just like being on the *Sultana*. It was basically seven paces to the windless, accounting for the need to climb around the gig that lay across the ship, just where the *Sultana* kept her second boat. The crew of the *Gaspee* ignored Bruce, and he was soon finished. He proceeded back to report to the lieutenant, noticing on the way some different choices in how she was rigged in contrast to the *Sultana*. When called in after knocking, Bruce saw a more cluttered cabin than Inglis's, and it appeared that they hadn't seen the need to move the bread room aft, like Inglis had.

"I inspected the anchor line, Lieutenant, and it is unserviceable," reported Bruce, after a quick salute.

"Exactly as I said. I really do not have time for this constant looking into my affairs by those higher up. Every moment I am here I am not uncovering contraband. I resent having to treat them with civility. Given the chance, I will seize smugglers and treat them for what they are—pirates!"

"Well, I —err, I will agree that many are incorrigible and insubordinate. But pirates? They are our countrymen . . . " Bruce said.

"Countrymen?! Bah—we might as well be at war with these bumpkins. At least that is how I look at it. And anything we need, I take, as spoil if you will. Some may object—and some have to my face—but I've taken sheep, hogs and chickens from the local farmers, and I am entirely in my rights to have done so. I've even had my men cut down their fruit trees for firewood.

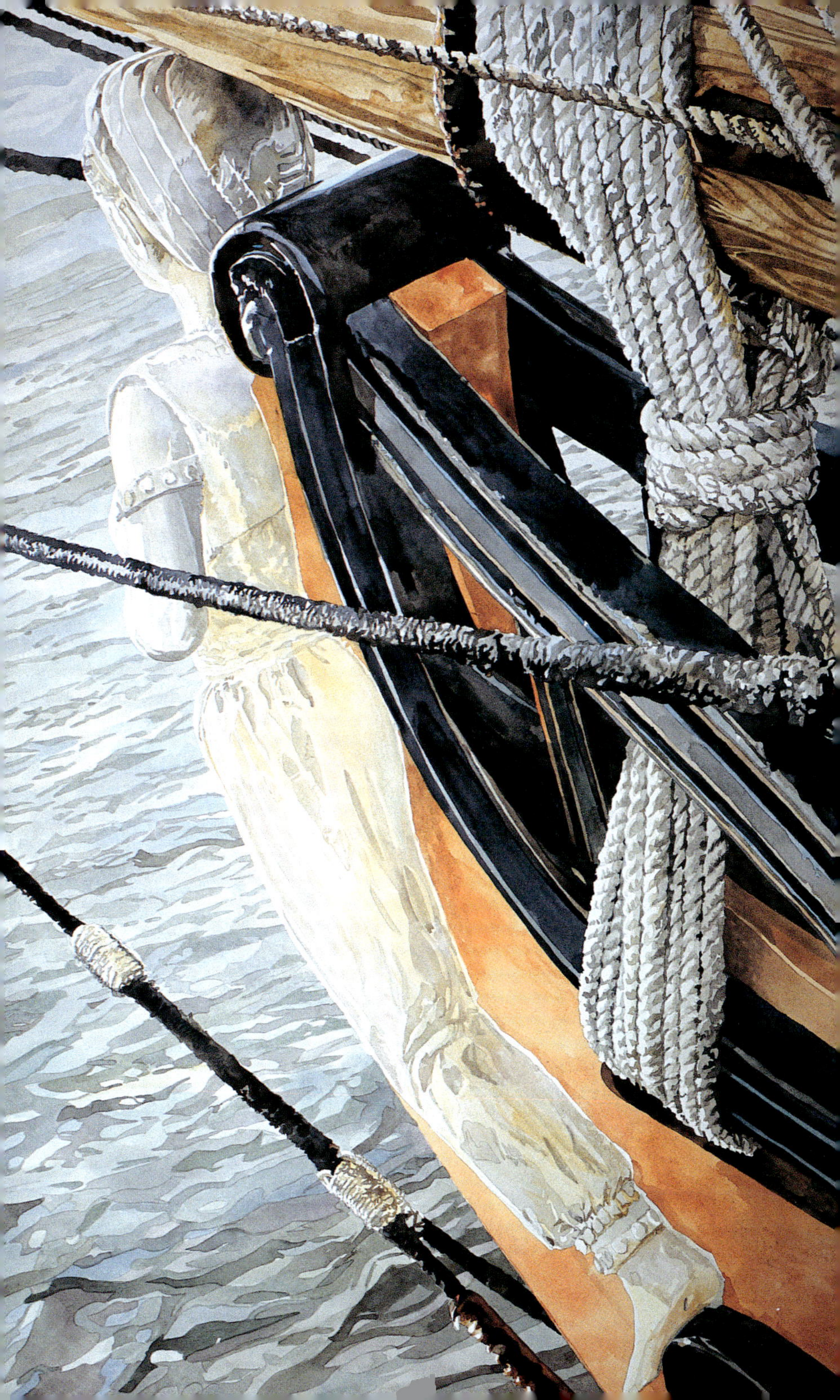

We must come down hard on these ungrateful cretins and their merchant vessels. They must know their place."

Such a blatant abuse of power in carrying out their common duties by such an obnoxious braggart jarred Bruce. Now, after having met Dudingston, Bruce was potently reminded that the colonists did not have a corner on blackguards. The lieutenant so annoyed Bruce that the dam set in his heart against the colonists broke, and he suddenly found a desire to defend them flooding over him.

"As I have had opportunity to dine with some of His Majesty's subjects here in the colonies," Bruce said, "they have communicated to me that they knew their 'place.' And that place was as loyal British citizens, subject to the King and the Constitution. The more level headed amongst them are clearly only looking to retain their British rights and have their grievances addressed through the system."

"Dined with them—in a pig's trough, perhaps? No, I am sure none in this region would even be able to set *that* fine of a table," scoffed Dudingston.

Bruce thought back to dining with Washington and the decency, dignity and decorum that pervaded that evening. He would choose to be a pig any day if his trough was as well furnished and abundantly stocked as Washington's table had been. His host that evening had spoken so courteously and respectfully to Bruce—basically just a common sailor—that he felt himself rise above his rank and carry himself as more of a gentleman. The contrast between the colonel and this braggart was so stark that he nearly laughed. But he was saved from having to suppress such an outburst because Dudingston abruptly finished the meeting by saying, "Good day to you, sir. Give my best to the *Sultana's* lieutenant—and don't go soft on these backwater pirates!" and returned to his papers.

Bruce returned to his launch and left the *Gaspee*, full of polar ideas and contrary emotions.

INGLIS LOGBOOK:

July 23, 1771 Anchored off New Castle on Delaware. Hard gales & squally weather with rain. At noon sailed hence His Majesty's Ship Rose & Gaspey schooner. Sent the Master on board the Gaspey to assist in surveying her cable per order of Captain Keeler.

July twenty-fifth marked the arrival of several more of the Royal Navy's finest, including the HMS *Mercury*, the HMS *Gibraltar* and the HM Schooner *Magdelan*. Along with the HM Schooner *Sultana*, they were a small but impressive fleet. Certainly, there were no thoughts of smuggling in Delaware's waters that day, even with the absence of the HMS *Rose*—having taken her leave two days earlier.

On the twenty-seventh, the *Sultana* sailed out of New

Castle. The *Sultana* and *Deal Castle* worked together for the next two weeks, searching ships in the harbor of New York before returning to the Delaware River. They found that stopping ships to search them was becoming a much more violent undertaking than it had been the first three years of their tour. Inglis and Bruce were calling for muskets to be shot more and more to stop ships, and they started September by having to fire the swivel guns at a ship from Liverpool to make her stop and haul down a pendant she had impudently hoisted.

Then in the beginning of September a rare event occurred in the recapture of a deserter. Two deserters, in fact—Henry Black and Robert Whaley. Both were given two dozen lashes with the cat-o-nine tails for attempting to desert. Black had been pressed into the *Sultana's* crew that July, while Whaley had already received two dozen of the best for theft.

INGLIS LOGBOOK:

September 10, 1771. Anchored off New Castle on Delaware. Light breezes with Cloudy & rain. At 4 pm Read the Articles of War to the Schooner's Company. Punished Henry Black & Robert Whaley with 2 dozen lashes each for absenting themselves from their duty & attempting to run away.

In the beginning of October the *Sultana* was sent up to Boston for a few weeks. On their return trip to Philadelphia to patrol the Delaware River for the winter, David Bruce found himself wiling away some time off duty, playing cards with the ship's clerk.

"So Will, what is the news about Boston?" Bruce asked as he dealt the first hand of Bone-Ace. "Somehow I was unable to get into the city the entire time we were in port."

"You were busy, weren't you?" answered Dearl as he shifted on the barrel he was sitting on to get more comfortable. "You didn't miss much in Boston, really. Mostly gossip about the replacement of Commodore Gambier back in August." The two men had set up their game just outside of Bruce's cabin, using the shot locker as a table for their game.

"Still? I thought that might be old news by now."

"No, the reasons for Gambier's extremely short time in Hood's old post have come to light. He was replaced primarily due to his generosity with the Navy's money. He set up a navy hospital in Boston and was offering bonuses to sailors who volunteered. He was trying to curb the need for press gangs. And I must tell you, with my experience clerking in the Navy, I've learned that blood flows more freely from stones than money out of the British Admiralty."

"The hospital was a good thing to do, even if he got in trouble for it, but trying to end press gangs is just madness. It won't work. But perhaps Montague our new Vice Admiral of the Blue has pockets deep enough to make such an idea sane. You know don't you, that Montague's cousin is Lord John Montague, the fourth Earl of Sandwich? He should ask him for enough money to stop the press," Bruce said, laughing at the absurdity of the notion.

"Let us set aside Gambier and Montague to talk of news closer to home—our own smitten Mr. Jurd."

"Ah yes, how is Jurd's long-haired chum?" Bruce asked.

"She's a peach. A sweet girl and possibly the most alluring I've seen in the colonies. If John weren't such a good-hearted lad, I'd have to hate him for his good fortune."

"Aye, a curvaceous and comely girl—but she'd talk a leg off a horse," Bruce interjected.

"That doesn't seem to bother Jurd—yesterday he summoned up the courage to ask the father for the girl's hand!"

"Good for John—perhaps on one of our next visits to Boston Inglis could grant him some time for a bit of a honeymoon before coming back on board . . ."

"Ah, there's the rub. The father is against the marriage—he is questioning John's declarations of devotion. He seems to think if John really wanted to marry his daughter that he'd give up life at sea for her."

"That is all well and good, but the *Sultana* is not going to give John up quickly—not with how reliable he is. A quality, for that matter, which would bode well for him marrying. I think he'd be the faithful sort. He'd be a better catch than you, that is certain . . . you can't even play a decent game of cards," Bruce teased, as he laid down his winning hand. "That's the third time in a row I've beat you."

The *Sultana* arrived off Glocester Point on the twenty-first of October. The crew diligently conducted their searches over the next month, boarding ship after ship in a marathon of engagements but uncovering no illegal shipments. Perhaps their unflagging labors were finally paying off and the colonists were conforming to the wishes of the Crown or they were smuggling out of other ports—it was difficult to know for sure. Nevertheless, the *Sultana* was able to have some measure of success at this time in adding to the number of their crew. The *Sultana* had been losing crew at a steady rate over the last several months due to desertion, but two joined in Philadelphia, including forty-three-year-old Andrew Mears from Donegal, Ireland.

Four days after adding the old Irish sailor Mears, the *Sultana* was sailing up the Delaware at noon and was hailed by the *King George*—the Philadelphia custom house's schooner.

An anchor line lay listlessly halfway down to the water, its end severed as the *King George* drifted about the Delaware. In addition to the lost anchor, the rigging had been cut and the deck was a heap of broken wood and blood. The *Sultana* anchored nearby and Inglis sent the cutter over manned with Bruce, Haliburton and many well-armed sailors.

"Master David Bruce of His Majesty's Schooner *Sult*—sweet Providence, sir, what happened?" Bruce gasped as they got on board.

"We were attacked last night by men wishing to liberate a boat we had seized," said the captain of the *King George*. "Please, send your surgeon over in all haste—I have badly hurt men that need care."

"Our man Haliburton is aft there, already at his task," Bruce said. "Jurd, McKenzie, Beck—begin cleaning away the wreckage on deck. Grant, Beck and the rest of you lads help our surgeon's mate with the wounded." The sailors began moving broken barrels and crates and attempting to tie down lines. They soon found that the custom house's schooner was badly damaged—much more than had been apparent as they approached her—and her entire crew was bruised and bleeding.

Bruce took the other end of a large smashed crate from the captain, "Thank you for your help, Master Bruce. My name is Muskett."

"Glad to be of service to you, sir. Our jobs have been getting more and more fierce in the past months, but I declare, this looks more like the work of Rhode Islanders than something I'd expect to see in the Delaware."

"I have never been so cruelly treated. I was quite unprepared for it," confessed Captain Muskett. "We searched a boat yesterday and found it filled with illegal wine and tea. We were taking her into custody when the wind died completely, forcing us to anchor. As we waited for the wind to spring up, a group of boats rowed out most heavily armed and caught us unaware. They took the vessel we had seized and brutally attacked me and my crew. The fury of their offensive left us almost immediately flat on deck, beaten and bloodied. Before they sailed off with their reclaimed prize, they threw us in the hold, fastened down the hatches and then cut our cables and anchors.

"These are dark days, sir," Bruce said grimly as the chaos inflicted on the *King George* and her crew deeply disheartened him. "When Haliburton has taken care of your men, we will tow you back to Philadelphia."

Inglis Logbook:

November 24, 1771 Anchored off Gloster point. Light airs with calms. At 11 am Boarded a Schooner from Boston in Ballast, at 12 the Custom house Boat came by & hail'd the schooner. Requested our assistance Acquainting us how they had made a seizure of a Pilot boat with prohibited goods, and some time after they took her into Custody a boat mann'd, & arm'd came & rescued the said boat & goods from them, Sent the boat mann'd & arm'd to their assistance

The winter of '71–'72 was the most brutal of their entire tour of the colonies. Work on board the ship was kept to the minimum—snow removal and making spun yarn. Toward the middle of December, able-bodied seaman John Brenson contracted smallpox. John Haliburton found there was little he could do to help Brenson, but he was able to protect the rest of the crew by making scratches and small cuts on the arms of each seaman, then rubbing pustular matter obtained from Brenson's sores into the open wounds. Although the other crewmen were spared, Brenson was buried in a Philadelphia church graveyard on the nineteenth of December.

Then the Delaware River froze over and didn't open until the last week of February 1772. At the end of the month, the weather turned bad once more—so much that no work was done at all on the *Sultana*. The merciless ice squeezed the small schooner to such an extent that they began emptying the hold to avoid being crushed.

Carolina

MARCH ROARED IN AND SENT MORE snow and ice on the *Sultana*, not relenting until the middle of the month. Smaller boats began to be searched for contraband as the servants of the Crown began to realize that foreign ships were unloading parts of their cargo into smaller craft before coming into port.

Yet as bad as the year began, it would only get worse.

On the first Thursday of that April, the *Sultana* caught up with the *King George*, which had a schooner in tow that she had discovered was smuggling twelve quarter casks of claret.

"Lieutenant Inglis! Might you be of assistance?" Captain Muskett's master hailed. "We intended to send a crew aboard this schooner, the *Betsy*, to take her in—she is smuggling claret—yet they protest." The crew of the *King George* had recovered from their wounds obtained the previous fall, but they looked as if they feared a repeat performance of that bloody drama.

"Only too glad to help," Inglis called back. "Master Bruce, take some of our crew, well-armed, with you over in the cutter. I will try to persuade the *King George's* quarry from here."

"Yes, sir," Bruce answered. "Grant, Black, Whaley—come with me," he called out as he went to carry out his orders.

"Nichollson," barked Inglis, "fire four half-pound cannon at the *Betsy*—at your earliest convenience. And try not to destroy the *George's* prize," he ordered with a wink.

The sound of the swivel guns being fired ate up the sky as Master Bruce and his band rowed over in the cutter. They rounded the *Betsy* to find some of her crew emptying into that schooner's tender. "Back up on deck, you lot!" Bruce called out as his men immediately raised their muskets. As they cocked their weapons, Bruce added, "I know rats are the first to desert a sinking ship, but don't worry—we will get you to shore without you getting wet." Bruce was finding his duty more and more onerous of late and found predictable simpletons like these just exaggerated the folly of it all.

The tide soon turned, literally, and the next day *Sultana* accompanied the two ships up the river until they were in sight of Philadelphia. The Delaware continued to flow with wine all month, as the *Sultana* later seized a boat carrying forty-five quarter casks of Malaga wine, six quarter casks of brandy, and twenty-seven kegs of rum.

INGLIS LOGBOOK

April 2, 1772 Anchored off Gloster Point. Strong gales and cloudy weather with rain, at 3 pm the Custom house schooner came up with us with a schooner they had stopt for having on board 12 Quarter Cask of Claret, and crav'd our assistance, Weigh'd and anchored close to her. Fired away to bring to 4 half pounders. Sent the boat on board her but would not let the boat board her till they given their muskets over them. The men took to their boat being afraid of being prest (!), our boat went on board. Came to anchor alongside the said schooner waiting for the tide to go up to the Custom house.

The wind was gusting and the *Sultana* had augmented her front jibsail with two more jibsails in order to gain the most momentum possible in her pursuit of the brig *Carolina*. Dearl, while in town resupplying the schooner, had heard that the brig was a known smuggler. Inglis was in great spirits at the thought of a prize nearly in his grasp.

"It is ironic, Master Bruce, that our clerk's informant would send us to Marcus Hook in pursuit of these renegades," Inglis said jauntily. "It was a Mr. Cain, wasn't it Dearl?"

"Indeed it was, sir," replied the ship's clerk.

"Where's the irony in that?" asked Bruce. He was feeling cold to the *Sultana's* duties, but the day's pursuit and near surety of financial gain was beginning to warm him to his responsibilities.

"Pirates! When I was a child in Philadelphia, it was often told that Blackbeard and his crew used to visit a certain cove along the Delaware—or *hoek* as the Dutch would say—and conduct wild drunken revels at the house of a Swedish woman whom he was accustomed to call Marcus," the Lieutenant gayly lectured. "And here we are not eight miles away from Marcus Hook, where today the brig *Carolina* is conducting a nefarious business with local scoundrels around the sale of contraband wines."

"That is until we get there and break up their party," Bruce rejoined.

"Precisely!" Inglis said, then added almost to himself, "We really need to make the most of this steadily rising wind at our back." Turning to the midshipman, he ordered, "Have the rear staysail hanked out, Mr. Piddle."

"Hank out the rear staysail," Piddle repeated and then passed the orders on to the sailors who would actually execute them.

The topsails danced prettily, and the schooner was cracking on—her twelve knots felt like twenty along the narrow banks of the Delaware River. Her wake churned white while across the breasts of the *Sultana's* figurehead was laid a foamy sash of brackish spray. The *Carolina* was soon in sight, and it seemed that they might be able to swoop down on their prey without warning. But the brig was on the lookout for all the King's men, and it wasn't long before the crew of the *Sultana* heard a faint cry of "Sail Ho" drift over the water, and they knew they were off to the races. The *Carolina* soon had her sails set, and they set out on a due southwesterly course. The breeze continued to freshen, and in spite of the *Carolina* leading the way, Inglis put a watch forward to guard against sandy shoals—the plague of the Delaware inlet.

"Take us due south," Inglis said to the helmsman as they reached the mouth of the river. "We should be able to blanket the *Carolina*." Inglis was betting that the brig was still full of her contraband cargo and thus would be slower and heavier on the water. Yet each time the *Sultana* made the move to head upwind, the *Carolina* feinted southwesterly, threatening to run the westerly side of the inlet.

"Any sign of Ship John's?" Inglis called forward, referring to the massive banks of shoals near the mouth of the inlet.

"No, sir," the sailor answered, "But I think the *King George* is headed this way!"

Bruce had his spyglass handy and confirmed the sighting, "She *is* the *King George*."

"Certainly I wish them all the best—but we're not sharing our prize with them today!" Inglis sent the men of the *Sultana* scurrying all over the ship, adjusting the sails to squeeze out every ounce of performance they could muster so as to overtake the *Carolina*.

The sailors and the schooner worked in well-nigh perfect harmony, and they were soon abreast of the brig.

"Nichollson, prepare to fire our chasers across her aft deck," Inglis called out. Then, just as the gunner's mate was returning to deck with powder, the chase abruptly ended. Apparently, the *Carolina* had seen the *King George* and knew she was bottled up between her, the shoals and His Majesty's smallest schooner.

"Mr. Piddle," Inglis ordered, "take six men over to the *Carolina* to search her." The midshipman chose the sailors to accompany him and was rowing over to the captured brig as the *King George* finally joined them. The men of the *Sultana* uncovered empty wine and brandy casks. They seized the *Carolina* and the three ships soon began the laborious process of tacking back up the river, with Piddle leading the prize crew on the *Carolina*.

As they approached the hook where they had originally found the *Carolina,* the wind began to fall off, the sky began spitting, and a raucous crowd formed on shore. Even without being able to decipher their words across the water, it was clear they were preparing to attack the *Sultana*.

"It appears that the *Carolina* has some friends," Bruce

said ruefully.

"And obviously they intend to use violence to prove their misguided devotion," Inglis replied. All the joy of the chase had left him as he called again for their gunner's mate. "Nichollson, load six swivel cannon with grape shot. We will squelch this rescue attempt immediately."

The tide seemed to be working in the *Sultana's* favor as the mob struggled to get boats out to the schooner. But before Nichollson received the order to fire on the vociferous horde, the King's schooner's were joined unexpectedly by the HMS *Lively*.

It has been said of the HMS *Lively* that she was "a crack frigate: her sailing qualities were quite out of the ordinary...." And certainly she had arrived so quickly this day that her reputation remained unimpeachable. She was over one hundred and fifty feet in length, had a crew just shy of three hundred, and boasted twenty-eight eighteen-pound long guns, four nine-pound long guns and over a dozen 32-pound carronades. Seeing her, the rowdy colonists immediately gave up their fight against the tide and relinquished their claim on the *Sultana*. And though the *Sultana* did not relinquish her claim to the *Carolina*, she did give her over to the *Lively's* Captain George Talbot to take her safely to the City of Brotherly Love.

INGLIS LOGBOOK:

May 8, 1772. Delaware River. Strong Gales and Squally. Going down the River in pursuit of the Brig that brought in Prohibited Wine. In Company with the King George Customhouse boat. Boarded the said Brig, and found on board her some empty wine & brandy Casks. Seized her on Suspicion.

Six days after the *Carolina* incident, able-bodied seaman Henry Black was lost overboard while he and several of the crew were boarding to search the sloop *Sally* from Jamaica. His clothes were auctioned off at the mast. Like most of the men on board, Black had not known how to swim. His body was washed up on shore almost two weeks later and found by a band of *Sultana's* crew who were on wood-gathering duty.

Black was nearly forty years old when he died, and Bruce knew he had had a fairly typical—though rather long—life, as sailors go. But when the crewmen brought his discolored and bloated body aboard, he was suddenly struck by the tragedy of it all. If they hadn't caught him back in September after he ran, the old scotsman might still be alive today. But instead he was caught, whipped and put back into the service of the Crown so that he could give up his life—and for what? To search a ship to see if they had any undeclared tea aboard? A feeling of meaninglessness engulfed him.

In June the *Sultana* broke up their nigh two month patrol of the Delaware Bay with a short vacation of about a week off Cape May. Cape May had first been seen in the same year that the Pilgrims landed at Plymouth, when a Dutch tradesman, Cornelius Jacobsen Mey, explored the coast of New Jersey and the Delaware River. On his voyage he found an island later to be known as Long Beach, and dubbed an inlet to the bay there "Barendegat" (literally, "Inlet of the Breakers"), before continuing down to the cape at the mouth of the Delaware River, a cape which he named after himself. Captain Mey was known to have once said, "Tis better to govern by love and friendship than by force," but the *Sultana* was able to govern neither by love nor friendship nor by force, due to unusually rough weather. The always beautiful region was hidden under rain and buffeted by a mad battering of heavy winds. It got so bad that by Saturday the *Sultana* was unable to board and search any vessels entering the waterway.

The rain beat mercilessly against the closed deadlights of the Lieutentant's cabin. "Well, David, it doesn't look like I will be able to get ashore during our time here."

Bruce turned from the logs he was working on and replied, "Why did you want to go ashore? I thought all that was here were whalers and farmers who fancied themselves pilots."

Inglis laughed. "The way they compete with each other, speeding out to get the job to guide vessels safely through these waters, I would fear to see the state of their farms! But there is more on Cape May Island than that. There are three taverns—the most prominent being owned and operated by Memucan Hughes. He is from one of the thirty-five founding families on the cape—they own most of the land in this region and regularly intermarry to keep it that way."

"They must be fine taverns if you wanted to go to the trouble of reaching them in this kind of storm."

"No, David, I wanted to go over to Cold Spring. People have been coming down there from Philadelphia since the 40's when the pastor of Cold Spring Presbyterian Church encouraged visitors to come to the natural cold spring there for their health. I never came down as a boy, but many I knew had. So since I was here, I thought I'd visit the spring."

"In this downpour, even if you were able to row to land,

I'm sure you'd have to swim to reach the spring—and that would certainly *not* be good for your health!" Bruce said, referring to Inglis's lack of swimming ability.

So the crew of the *Sultana* missed out on enjoying the Cape's lovely swells of soft white sand dunes covered in salt meadow and seashore elder. A whale's tail was sighted, but mostly the men were busying themselves with routine maintenance like mending the seine net for fishing, helping the carpenter repair the bilge pumps or helping Nichollson clean the small arms. John Jurd, however, spent the whole time fretting to his mates about the honeymoon he was afraid would never come.

INGLIS LOGBOOK:

June 6, 1772 Anchor'd under Cape May. Hard gales & rain, some vessels enter'd the Capes but could not board them on account of the Weather & Sea.

Gaspee

*B*Y THE FIFTEENTH OF THE MONTH THEY were back in the Philadelphia area on the Delaware under fair skies and fine breezes. But the weather in Cape May had been more of an indicator of the mood in the colonies, especially to the north.

The *Sultana* fired at several small vessels that day to bring them to. And it was on one carrying lumber that Master Bruce boarded that day that news of great weight was passed on.

"You Navy Royal tars fire on all your countrymen these days, eh?" a sour captain accused Master Bruce as he and his men boarded the *Alexandra* to search her.

"Captain McMullen, His Majesty's Schooner *Sultana* is enforcing the laws of the Crown, and if doing so requires firing off a warning shot or two, then that is what we have to do," Bruce answered.

"Maybe you'll think twice about shooting at us in the future after what happened to the *Gaspee*."

"I'm afraid I don't follow you. Now about your cargo—"

"You mean you haven't heard?"

"No—we've been on the Delaware for quite some time. The *Gaspee* is patrolling around Newport," Bruce replied distractedly, then instructing his men, "Jurd, McKenzie . . . give Mears help moving around the lumber down there in the hold. We need to be able to look under it."

"*Was* patrolling. The *Gaspee* was run aground and burned to the waterline."

"It cannot be," Bruce replied, his attention captured. Instinctively he took a glance at the *Sultana* to make sure she hadn't been burned to the waterline in his absence. This news stuck him at his core due to the similarities between the two boats, as well as all the times colonists had threatened the *Sultana*.

"Indeed, it is true. The news is all over the city. The way I heard it when I was down at the Rose Tree Tavern was that the commander of the *Gaspee* was enforcing the trade laws with an inordinate amount of relish—even seizing rowboats. And he was in the habit of *firing at the Providence ships*," said the captain with a pointed look, "to compel them to salute his flag by lowering theirs as they passed by."

"Which is only right," Bruce interjected defensively. "We've done the same."

"Then he'd chase them into the docks if they did not comply."

"Hmmm, yes, that is a bit farther than we have pursued mending the breach of etiquette ourselves," admitted Bruce. Though he couldn't say he was surprised. After his own encounter with the *Gaspee's* Lieutenant Dudingston, he realized nothing was beyond the scope of possibility with that arrogant lowlife.

"Less than a week ago the *Hannah* was conveying passengers to Providence and was fired at by the *Gaspee* for not paying the King's schooner the proper respect. The *Gaspee* gave chase and the *Hannah* took advantage of the high tide to run close to the shore. The *Gaspee* took the bait and ran aground! The *Hannah* proceeded in glory to Providence, where the story quickly spread and a plot was hatched to destroy the obnoxious vessel."

"There is a fearsome number of angry people in that town. We had a run in with those folks last year in just the same spot," a slightly mollified Bruce cut in.

"The ring leader was John Brown, that prosperous merchant who was such a vocal opponent of the Stamp Act," said the man. "Whipple, a ship-master, joined him in this action, and together they rounded up sixty-four armed and determined men. They set off in whale-boats at two o'clock the next morning and boarded the *Gaspee* so quickly that her crew was immediately subdued.

"How many were killed or injured? We came to the aid of the *King George* after such an incident and the whole boat was bathed in blood," said Bruce.

"It was nothing like that mate. Only Dudingston was hurt—a musket ball shot to the groin," laughed the small vessel's captain. "After the Rhode Islanders had command of the *Gaspee*, they took the Lieutenant ashore—together with his private effects and his crew—and torched the schooner. Of course, a Commission of Inquiry has been set up in Rhode Island, but it seems that all the Newport residents have had a convenient loss of memory about the attack," he said with a sly smile.

"This isn't just rioters getting carried away in the heat of the moment, this armed action smacks of outright war," Master Bruce concluded. True, Bruce admitted to himself, he couldn't think of anyone else in the world he would rather see take a musket ball to the groin... but this action changed all the rules for the Royal Navy patrolling the North American waterways.

"Well, I don't know about war, but—hey, watch what you're doing there!" the *Alexandra's* captain turned suddenly to call down to the *Sultana's* men in the hold. "I can bear the search of my ship, but I'll not stand for you making the hold a stew! There is nothing amiss here—my paperwork matches the cargo. This whole shipment came from the Pratt plantation by barge down Ridley Creek. Joseph and Jane Pratt are busy trying to raise their seven children—they won't be dabbling in smuggling." The men of the *Sultana,* chastised, straightened up after themselves and set the *Alexandra* on her way. But Bruce was in a daze until he came back aboard their schooner, where he shared the dark news of the *Gaspee* with Inglis.

Inglis Logbook:

June 15, 1772 Anchor'd off Chester Town Moderate breezes and fair weather. Boarded and Rummaged several small vessels in the boat from different parts of the River with Corn, Lumber, & Shingles. Fired away to bring to said vessels.

Note: The "Chester Town" in this entry is present-day Chester, Pennsylvania.

The rest of the summer was spent on the Delaware River in the company of the *King George* and the *Lively.* July began with the unexpected treat of *Lively* distributing to the men aboard the *Sultana* their one and only pay of prize money.

INGLIS LOGBOOK:

July 9, 1772 Anchor'd off Chester Moderate & clear Weather. At 3 pm Weigh'd, & came to sail going down to Chester to join HMS Lively. People employ'd scraping the sides and paying them with turpentine. Paid the people their seizure money.

In the middle of August their ranks swelled by one with the return of a healthy midshipman, but desertions continued to plague the schooner, requiring that more men be pressed from the merchant ships they searched. After the impress of their last sailor, William Helm, a weary Inglis told Bruce over a brandy in the Lieutenant's cabin, "Filling our ranks is a tiresome business. Did I ever tell you about my initial experience with having to press? I took the first day I ever pressed a man no less than 150 seamen, the crews of three East Indiamen. But I pray to Heaven never to be witness to such a scene again, for I never felt half so much distress after an engagement as I did from the sorrowful countenances of a parcel of poor fellows dragged away

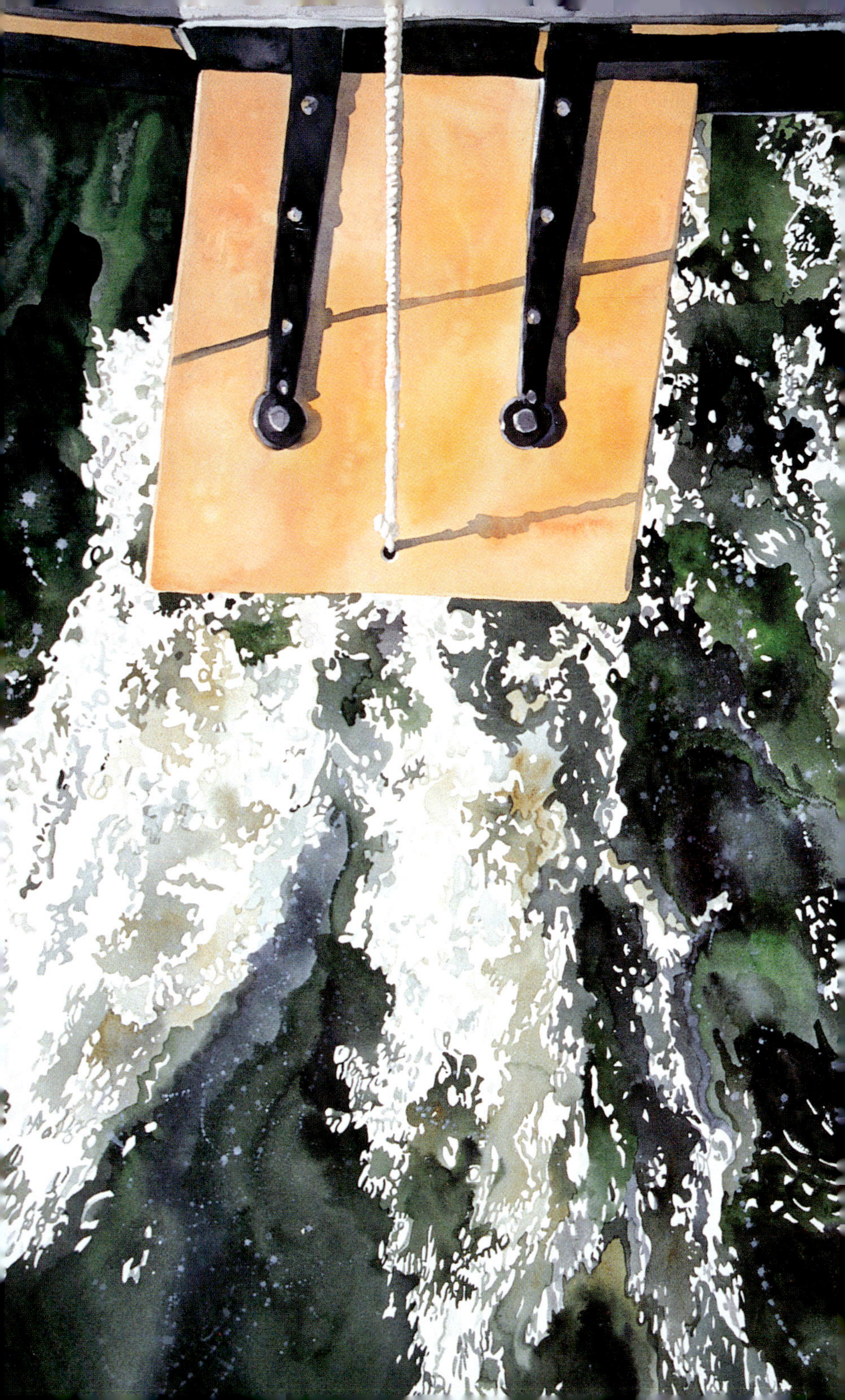

against their will. But tho' I feel for anyone forced under the rigor of the Articles of War, yet there will be this consolation to those that have been brought under my command: that they will experience all the mildness and tenderness they can reasonably expect."

"Well, if you thought it was the wrong thing to do, why did you do it?" asked Bruce.

"David, you've said so yourself—the press is a fact of life."

"Yes, I know I have, but perhaps there are times when we need to take a stand against what is wrong in the world."

"The Navy needs to stay manned—we have our duty to perform," Inglis offered as justification.

"Our duty! And as I carry out that duty, I wonder if God shouldn't *'justly damn me for the best duties that ever I did perform?'*" Bruce said, as unexpected emotion started to color his voice.

"Where did you get that?" Inglis replied.

"That preacher, Whitefield, said it. But the point is, maybe there are things that outrank duty."

"I do my best to see that the right thing is done within the constraints of my position. Like I said, those brought under my command are shown every kindness. I care for each one—"

"Really? *Each* one? What about Fitzgerald?"

"Who—?"

"John Fitzgerald ... he died two Aprils ago; we were on the Elizabeth River near Point Comfort."

"Oh, yes, Fitzgerald—why bring him up?"

"The man died under your command, and you didn't even make a passing reference to it in your log," Bruce said emphatically.

"I didn't? Oh well, he was only an Irishman and never seemed that loyal to the Crown."

"Loyalty that ignores right and wrong is damning regardless of how well-meaning it is," Bruce asserted.

"I—that is, the way I see it is . . .," Inglis stammered. Then his face blanched but his charcoal eyes darkened, "Well, right now, Master Bruce, I believe you have a duty to perform on deck."

"Yes, Lieutenant," Bruce said, turning on his heel to climb the ladder to go topside.

Inglis Logbook:

September 3, 1772 Cape May WbS 7 Leagues Fresh gales & clear weather. At 4 pm weigh'd, and came to sail, going down the River, for Boston per order. Got the boat in, set the topsails and square sail. Swim'd on shore one man in the night.

The *Sultana* received orders on the first of September to sail to Boston in preparation for a return trip to England. On the ninth the *Sultana* arrived in Boston, giving Rear Admiral Montagu on the *Fowley* a 13-gun salute. Once anchored, they prepared for the return passage to England, replacing cables, repairing the fishing seine and refreshing their food stocks.

"John," Bruce said matter-of-factly, "you are going to accompany Mr. Dearl ashore for food, but first the Lieutenant asked to see you." He followed Jurd below to Inglis's cabin and ushered the nervous seaman in before closing the door between them.

"Sir?" Jurd saluted the Lieutenant.

"John, you have served the Crown and this schooner very well," Inglis stated coolly. "You were one of the first to enlist with *Sultana* as she worked her way down the English Channel over four years ago. I want to thank you for your loyalty."

"Thank you, sir," a nervous Jurd answered.

"Though I am told by Mr. Dearl that you have chronically taken a great deal of extra time when getting bread for the *Sultana* from the Boston bakers," Inglis queried with mock sternness before breaking into a smile and saying, "Mr. Dearl told me of your request to stay here in Boston. The Royal Navy is honoring your petition—you are hereby discharged."

Jurd stood there in silence as his eyes began to mist, threatening to storm. All he choked in reply was, "Thank you, sir."

Jurd found Bruce waiting for him outside the master's cabin. "Go get married and have a wonderful life in these backwater colonies," Bruce said, slapping the sailor on the back. "Though if you'll ever have a moment's peace and quiet with that girl, it will be a miracle!"

Boston 8th October 1772

The Sultana Schooner having been out of England upwards of Five years and is much out of repair, I have sent her home that her Company may be paid their Wages, and for their Lordships to dispose of her as they please. I beg you will inform their Lordships that the Schooner was Built for a pleasure Boat for a Gentleman at Southampton but not answering his purpose, she was purchased for Government by orders of Sir Edward Hawke, and sent out here, she is by no means fit for this Station being too small and not able to encounter the heavy Gales of wind upon this coast, especially in the Winter Season. But as Lieut Inglis has been in her most part of the time she has been in this Country, I beg leave to refer their Lordships for his Opinion & Character of her.

—Rear Admiral John Montagu
Chief of the North Atlantic Station

The *Sultana* continued to get restocked—without the aid of John Jurd—and on the eleventh of October set off for England, having made her last, fruitless inspection for contraband the previous day. The first week and a half of the trip was uneventful, which suited the weary sailors very well.

On October 23rd, as the men on duty were singing shanties while they trimmed the *Sultana* to her sailing best, they all were sharing their plans for what they'd do once they were paid off. Inglis and Bruce were getting along well once again, their recent contention smoothed over by common ship routine and extra effort by both parties. As Bruce was just about to climb the ladder up on deck for his watch, Inglis called out from his desk: "David, I was just reviewing the muster, and do you realize we have had over one hundred men serve on this vessel during these past four years?"

Bruce stopped and leaned against the ladder. "That many? I suppose I shouldn't be surprised, but with a tour of just four years, it does sound like a lot."

"I imagine it can be credited to the disease of the mind which the 'Sons of Liberty' and the other riff-raff gentry in the colonies are spreading."

"Certainly there are some distortions being circulated—I know I will never get over how that Adams fellow twisted that ruckus in Boston into a 'massacre,'" Bruce said. "But if there is one thing I learned from Jurd's bride it is that there are many issues on the table, and many of the colonists think Parliament is not ruling in the colonists' best interest or according to the rules laid out in their charters."

"I cannot fathom how they don't see that the Crown is protecting them from themselves," Inglis rejoined. "Just think how disastrous it would be if they were left to govern alone? They would find themselves under the rule of a set of desperate bad men, who would expose them in such a way as would best aggrandize their own wicked purposes."

"Washington doesn't fit that description," countered Bruce. "And the colonists don't see the Crown eager to protect them but rather as merely an opportunistic bully. I can appreciate how they might feel that they need a way of relief."

"The colonists are false and fickle half-wits who hold up treason as a virtue and loyalty as a vice."

"Again, I remember our host at Mount Vernon drinking to King George. He did not strike me as disloyal. Though he seemed to indicate that there were higher values at stake. Disloyalty is not always the greatest evil," David countered. Then a memory of a previous conversation with Inglis struck him to the core, and he added with fervor, "Why you yourself deserted rather than serving under someone you saw as a tyrant. Maybe Parliament is the colonies' HMS *Garland,* King George their Arbuthnot, and they should be jumping ship just like *you* did!"

Bruce's words hung in the cabin as all the sounds of water, wind, sailors and sails seemed to immediately go mute. The two officers stared in silence at each other with an unspoken understanding that an invisible line had been crossed in their journey, over which neither would return.

"This sounds like another piece of bad navigation, Mr. Bruce," the captain said, with no humor in his voice.

"No, *sir,* I don't think it is," Bruce replied softly. A wave of clarity had washed over the *Sultana's* master, and he began to plot a new course in his mind.

Perhaps Jurd had had it right, thought Bruce as he returned to deck. But as he turned and laid his hand on the binnacle, all plans for the future were blown from his mind as he noticed that the skies were beginning to darken and the waves to swell ominously. A storm was brewing, and David Bruce was none too happy about it.

Epilogue

On the twenty-third of October the *Sultana* encountered hard gales and squalls. It was particularly difficult sailing on that first day of the storm. A great deal of sea swept over the small schooner, filling the boat, knocking over the binnacle and washing over the cutter. This created a great drag on the *Sultana,* laying the schooner on her beam ends. Providentially, one of the crew was able to cut away the boat, allowing the schooner to right itself—saving the lives of all aboard. The soggy schooner sloshed it's way under stormy skies for the remainder of their crossing.

The *Sultana,* "very leaky in her bows," arrived in England early in December. She was given to the dockyard officers at the shipyard in Portsmouth, where she was emptied and all her rigging removed. Sixteen crew members—out of the one hundred men that had served on the *Sultana*—were paid off and transferred to other ships.

Lieutenant Inglis left the Royal Navy and spent some time in Scotland to recuperate. He would return to America in 1773 as master of the merchantman *St. George* for his brother's firm. Inglis returned to the Navy and was eventually promoted to Vice-Admiral of the Blue on November 9, 1805. He died of gout a little over two years later. There is no record of he and Master David Bruce ever serving together again.

Despite the damage received during the *Sultana's* tour of the colonies and hazardous return voyage, the shipwright at Portsmouth estimated that it would have cost only £70 to accomplish the "small repair to make good." But the Royal Navy decided she wasn't useful to them anymore. They auctioned her off on August 11, 1773, for a pitiful £85.

Acknowledgments

I would like to recognize and thank the following people: Chris Cerino for his generous aid, enthusiasm and answering of a million email queries for log entries facts verification; Drew McMullen for research aid via email too, as well as for his book and booklet which helped steer this project—and, of course, the tour of the *Sultana* he gave my family while it was under construction that inspired the writing of this book; Kees de Mooy for his papers concerning the exploits of the *Sultana*—this book could not have happened without them; Marc Porter for his paper (which, among other things, inspired this book's title), as well as his labors compiling the information from the muster books of *Sultana;* Marlin and Laurie Detweiler for catching the vision to do the *Veritas Maritime Series;* Bob Brown for a crash course in colonial religion; Lisa R. Smith and Eric Novotny for research assistance into George Whitefield; Mike Cain for his integral part in choreographing the naval maneuvers of the *Sultana* in this book; N.A.M. Rodger for his fabulous book; Master Chris and Captain Jamie for answers during a delightful sail; Marc Castelli for his beautiful artwork; Lucian Niemeyer for the photographs; Anne Weber for the priceless editing she did—she made a story out of a history report; Jessica Martin for writing advice; Mark Achtermann; Jim Wagner—Trunnelmeister and Master Gunner Emeritus; Dave Bustard for research assistance and encouragement. And, of course, most importantly, I thank my wife Leslie for her unwavering support during this project.

Selected Bibliography

de Mooy, Kees. "In Pursuit of Revenue: The Exploits of his Majesty's Armed Schooner *Sultana* 1768-1772," Washington College doctoral thesis.
—. "Living History: Diary of the Schooner *Sultana*." Washington College Magazine, Summer 2001.
—. "Loyal to the Crown: The Story of Sultana's Captain, Lieut. John Inglis," *Schooner Sultana Shipmates*, September 30, 2000.
Porter, Marc. "1,436 Days on the North American Station with the Crew of His Majesty's Schooner *Sultana*, October 24, 1768 to October 12, 1772." East Carolina University, December 9, 1999.
McMullen, Drew. *Schooner* Sultana: *Building a Chesapeake Legacy,* Tidewater Publishers, 2002.
—. "A Guide to the 1768 Reproduction Schooner *Sultana*," Sultana Projects, Inc., Chestertown, Md.
Rodger, N.A.M. *The Wooden World: An Anatomy of the Georgian Navy.* New York: Bancroft, 1981.

Glossary

Following is a listing of nautical terms, many of which are used in this book.

ABAFT Toward the rear (stern) of the boat. Behind.
ABEAM At right angles to the keel of the boat, but not on the boat.
ABOARD On or within the boat.
AFT Behind, or near the stern of the ship.
AGROUND Touching or fast to the bottom.
ALEE Away from the direction of the wind. Opposite of windward.
ALOFT Above the deck of the boat.
ANCHOR "To swallow the anchor" was slang for leaving the Navy.
ASTERN In back of the boat, opposite of ahead.
BATTEN DOWN Secure hatches and loose objects both within the hull and on deck.
BEAM The greatest width of the boat.
BEARING The direction of an object expressed either as a true bearing as shown on the chart, or as a bearing relative to the heading of the boat.
BEAT UP To sail in the direction from which the wind blows.
BELOW Beneath the deck.
BERTH A space for a ship to dock or anchor
BILGE The interior of the hull below the floor boards.
BILGE WATER water which collects in the bilges of a ship; if left, it soon acquires an offensive color of corruption. Nautical slang for rubbish or nonsense.
BITTER END The last part of a rope or chain.
BINNACLE A wooden case or box containing compasses, log-glasses, watch-glasses and lights to show the compass at night.
BOATSWAIN (pronounced BO'SUN) the officer responsible

for the rigging, sails and sailing equipment. The boatswain looks after the general working of the ship, especially with regard to anchors, cables, blocks and tackles.

BOW the front of the vessel

BRIG A two-masted vessel, mostly square-rigged, but with a fore-and-aft mainsail.

CAPSIZE To turn over.

CAREEN To beach and tilt a ship, exposing her bottom to allow the removal of marine growth.

CLEAT A fitting to which lines are made fast. The classic cleat is approximately anvil-shaped.

COCKET A certified document given to a shipper as a warrant that his goods have been duly entered and that duties have been paid.

CUTTER A ship's boat used for transporting stores or passengers.

DEAD LIGHTS A kind of shutter for the windows in the stern of a ship, used in very bad weather.

DEAD RECKONING Determining the ship's position by using only the ship's course indicated by its compass, the distance indicated by the log, and taking into account drift and leeway.

DOG WATCH One of the two two-hour watches between 4 and 8 p.m. The dog watches permit a shift in the order of the watch every 24 hours so that the same men will not have the same watch every night.

FATHOM Six feet.

FLIMSY A certificate describing the conduct of a midshipman, usually given to a midshipman by his commanding officer when he leaves an appointment.

FOLLOWING SEA An overtaking sea that comes from astern.

FORE-AND-AFT In a line parallel to the keel.

FORWARD Toward the bow of the boat.

GAFF A spar attached to the mast and used to extend the upper edge of a fore-and-aft sail.

GALLEY The kitchen area of a boat.

GIG A ship's boat.

GIVE CHASE To pursue a quarry.

Glossary

GROG A mixture of rum with water. In 1740 Admiral Vernon (known as "Old Grog" because of a grogram cloak he habitually wore) introduced the watering-down of the sailors' rum, and the beverage soon achieved the name of Grog.

GUNNER'S MATE Officer in charge of firearms and cannons.

HALF-HOGSHEADS A large barrel or cask capable of holding about thirty-six gallons of alcohol.

HARD TACK Hard, dried bread which does not deteriorate when stored on board ship for long periods of time. Also called ship biscuit.

HATCH An opening in a boat's deck fitted with a watertight cover.

HELM The wheel or tiller controlling the rudder.

HOLD A compartment below deck in a large vessel, used solely for carrying cargo.

HOVE DOWN When a ship is placed on shore for repairs.

HULL The part of the boat which sits in the water.

JIB A triangular sail set ahead of the foremost mast.

KEEL The part of the hull which sticks down lower in the water below the bottom of the hull to stop a boat from moving sideways.

KNOT A measure of speed equal to one nautical mile (6076 feet) per hour. Also, a fastening made by interweaving rope to form a stopper.

LARBOARD The left-hand side of a ship when facing forward. Also called port.

LAUNCH A ship's boat.

LAY To put oneself into the position indicated.

LEE The side sheltered from the wind.

LEEWARD The direction away from the wind. Opposite of windward.

LEEWAY The sideways movement of the boat caused by either wind or current.

LINE Rope and cordage used aboard a vessel.

MAST A vertical spar to which the fore-and-aft sails are attached.

MASTER The senior officer of a naval sailing ship in charge of routine seamanship and navigation but not in command during combat.

MIDSHIP Approximately in the location equally distant from the bow and stern.

MIDSHIPMAN A temporary rank held by young naval officers in training.

NAVIGATION The art and science of conducting a boat safely from one point to another.

PILOT One who, though not belonging to a ship's company, is licensed to conduct a ship into and out of port or through dangerous waters.

POOP The highest and aftermost deck of a ship.

PORT The left side of a boat looking forward. Also called larboard. A harbor.

RATLINE One of the small lines traversing the shrouds and forming rope ladders used by seamen for going aloft.

REEF To temporarily reduce the area of a sail exposed to the wind, usually to guard against adverse effects of strong wind or to slow the vessel.

REEFER An old naval name for a midshipman.

RIGGING The arrangement of masts, spars, and sails on a sailing vessel.

RUDDER A vertical plate or board for steering a boat.

SCHOONER A fore-and-aft rigged sailing vessel having at least two masts, with a foremast that is usually smaller than the other masts.

SCUTTLE A small opening or hatch with a movable lid in the deck or hull of a ship.

SEINE A large fishing net made to hang vertically in the water by weights at the lower edge and floats at the top.

SHROUD One of a set of strong ropes extending on each side of a masthead to the sides of a ship to support a mast laterally. Shrouds take their name from the spars they support.

SLOOP A single-masted, fore-and-aft-rigged sailing boat with a short standing bowsprit or none at all and a single headsail set

GLOSSARY

from the forestay.

SLOPS Articles of clothing and bedding issued or sold to sailors.

SPAR A wooden pole used to support sails and rigging.

SQUALL A sudden, violent wind often accompanied by rain.

STARBOARD The right side of a boat when looking forward.

STERN The after part of the boat.

STOW To put an item in its proper place.

STRIKE To haul down (a mast or sail) or to lower (a flag or sail) in salute or surrender.

SURGEON'S MATE Medical officer aboard ship.

TAR A sailor.

TACKLES A system of ropes and blocks for raising and lowering weights of rigging and pulleys for applying tension.

TENDER A vessel attendant on other vessels, especially one that ferries supplies between ship and shore.

TOPSAIL A triangular or square sail set above the gaff of a lower sail on a fore-and-aft-rigged ship

WAKE Moving waves, track or path that a boat leaves behind it when moving across the waters.

WAY Movement of a vessel through the water used in such terms as headway, sternway or leeway.

WINDLASS A lifting device consisting of a horizontal cylinder turned by a crank on which a cable or rope winds

WINDWARD Toward the direction from which the wind is coming.

YARDS A long, tapering spar slung to a mast to support and spread the head of a square sail.

The Schooner *Sultana*

The Schooner *Sultana* is an undertaking of Sultana Projects, Inc., a non-profit, 501(3)(c) organization based in Chestertown, Maryland. Founded in 1997, *Sultana's* mission is to provide unique, hands-on educational experiences in colonial history and environmental science. The principal classroom for *Sultana* is a full-scale reproduction of the 1768 colonial schooner *Sultana*.

The Schooner *Sultana* also offers public sails, public transit passages and charters. For more information call 410-778-5954 or email admin@schoonersultana.com.